Krista Wagner
Rian Field

Rian Field is a work of fiction. Though some of the situations are taken from the author's own experience, many of the relating incidents have been creatively reimagined for literary effect. Names of businesses and locations, though real, are used in a way that is purely fictional. Any similarity to actual persons, living or dead, is purely coincidental.

Published by CreateSpace, a DBA of
On-Demand Publishing, LLC

Cover Image by Adriana, freeimages.com

ISBN-13: 978-1523337941

ISBN-10: 152333794X

ASIN: B01AFF84CA

Printed in the United States of America

To my parents, for giving me life and love.

1

KRISTA WAGNER

RIAN FIELD

Chapter One

"There is the sea, great and broad,
In which are swarms without number,
Animals both small and great" Psalm 104:25

~November 1 2015~

The sun began its descent. Half of a sphere now drifting below the horizon, it burned dimly, a liquid ball of glowing fire soon to be dissolved by the impeding night.

To Rian Field's right, the 24 foot cruiser rocked gently atop the incipient waves of the Pacific Ocean, near the dock. The Sea Ray 230 Sundancer was powered by a 260hp, 5.7L Mercruiser, enhanced by a fiberglass-lined cockpit with a portside lounger, fish finder, VHF stereo, and a galley complete with mini fridge, marble countertops, and a microwave.

This was Rian's first experience in *Freedom* since she and her husband, Jack, purchased it a few weeks before. While Jack was an avid fan of the ocean, Rian had been a stranger to it until recently. She had been raised in Ft. Meade, Maryland, a daughter of two Air Force officers. Their families' outdoor ventures had been limited; she visited Ocean City, the nearest beach to the base, only once during her childhood. Now no longer deprived of the marine life, she anxiously stepped into the vessel and sat for a moment.

She wasn't fond of being out in the ocean. It was foreign to her. And she couldn't help but associate the movie *Jaws* with it—she both loved it and was terrified by it. But there was a strange irony to that fear. She had pursued a field that unavoidably and literally plunged her into the ocean. She received a PhD in Marine Estuarine & Environmental Sciences with a specialization in Ecology from University of Maryland Baltimore County. She chose ecology because it

3

kept her mostly on land. The study of human interaction within other ecosystems had always attracted her for reasons she didn't quite understand.

The best part of her schooling had been working in the lab conducting experiments on rare species. Many of her classmates avoided working in the lab, complaining of its monotony or the propensity for samples becoming contaminated. But where most saw predictable redundancy, Rian saw only mystery and intrigue.

Once she graduated, Rian spent most of her time researching terrestrial life—bears, deer, foxes, though recently she had shifted her focus to aquatic life where she had the opportunity to observe fish in their natural habitat. It was rewarding and terrifying at the same time for the same reason—it put her in close proximity to the Great White. Even in this environment, a lot of her partners grew bored or frustrated due to extreme weather conditions or the noncooperation of the fish. It wasn't as though they could schedule a meeting with sharks.

People often questioned her about her chosen field given the fact that she was wary of the ocean. She couldn't help it. Ever since she watched *Jaws* as a child, she'd become fascinated with sharks. Overall, it was the desire to find truth and to understand, or at least try to understand, the world that had drawn her to the sciences. She completed her studies with the expectation of working as a faculty member inside a facility, on land, not in the ocean. But some things had changed at Southern California Marine Institute (SCMI) where she worked.

Located near San Pedro in Terminal Island, about an hour from home in Newport Beach, the SCMI had turned out to be a place of opportunity. She had grown comfortable as a Professor of Biological Sciences, working with students and delivering lectures about sea life, happy with the work environment. It was safe being indoors. So while she was somewhat wary of the ocean world, it was mostly because she didn't know it, not in the physical sense, just academically. But then the director of the Institute, Westen Adams, decided it was time she commit to getting her feet wet in every sense of the word. Jack, always supportive, had been ecstatic about the news. Rian had been too. And nervous, of course.

Yet in all the months of exploring what was formerly an estuary, she hadn't once encountered anything of interest, much less anything exciting. As a Marine Biologist, she anticipated the discovery of a rare species or at least the detection of plankton that would lead her to an elusive mammal or fish. Instead, Rian found herself sailing the coastal area surrounded by nothing more than avid birdwatchers. She was starting to think that she should shift her attention to the university, researching the changes in aquaculture and going back to her earlier studies on ecosystems and their interaction with the climate. She felt comfortable in that environment.

She sighed, feeling a bit exhausted, and stood up to look out at the offing as the aquamarine sea transformed into a sheet of opaque glass underneath the falling sun. Maturing waves danced together as they rolled closer to the coast. Families, worn out by the earlier heat of the day, began packing their belongings and heading home, the sound of their voices fading with the sun. She smiled, looking forward to joining Jack for a nice and relaxing dinner at home.

To the west, the magenta sky released the sun of its daily obligation. She watched as tones of black gradually diffused over the last of the radiant hues of red and purple.

Rian looked around Balboa Island and realized she was all alone in this great body of water. The smile left her face. Maybe she should come back later. With Jack. She almost fell into the driver's seat as she attempted to sit down. She was more tired than she thought.

She was just about to turn off the engine when something slammed into the back of the vessel. The impact of the blow knocked into her with full force. She fell forward, her head colliding first with the metal steering wheel before she plunged to the carpeted floor.

A strange noise, something like a loud roar, pierced the air. She couldn't pull herself off the floor. Something warm and wet was running down her nose. It felt like a tear. Before she had time to react, a rush of water poured into the base of the boat. Cold spray tickled her face as she lied in a pool of salt water. Rian started to look toward the source of the commotion when the gel-coated stern began to splinter, then snap, until it collapsed into several jagged pieces as though they were made out of cheap plywood.

Another force of pressure plowed into the boat. Halfway to a standing position, Rian fumbled forward into the steering wheel again, this time bruising her chest. Stepping backward, she tried to regain her balance but was thrown once more against the wheel again as a monstrous force pushed the craft onward, at an impossible super speed, driving it past several docked boats until, ultimately, the Sundancer nosedived into the bay.

The splash of the turbulent waves gradually ceased. Balboa Island appeared strangely deserted, a sinister ghost town. Twilight gently embraced the island so that the harbor appeared like nothing more than a shelter of whispering surf.

Rian was lying on her back, her clothes soaked with water. She was certain death was near as thousands of little sparkling lights blackened her vision. Moaning softly, she attempted to move her left arm, but it remained limply at her side. Her head pounded with excruciating pain, and she became uncannily aware of a sharp ache materializing in the cavity of her chest. Her head was turned at a right angle. She managed to blink her eyes into focus once more. The stern of the cruiser had been completely torn free.

What's happened? Am I really alive?

As she reached up to touch her forehead, dark blood

started trickling down her face. She needed to apply pressure to the wound, but she couldn't move. She had to find a way out of the boat before she met her death or her husband and loved ones would be visiting her gravesite in the next few days. There was too much to live for still. Yet no matter how much she attempted to raise herself off the floor, she could find no physical strength to get up.

More blood oozed down her nose and into her mouth. She cringed at the coppery tang, but she couldn't take her eyes off the back of the boat.

Suddenly finding new strength, she pulled herself up into a sitting position, placing weight on her left leg, then her right, as she used the front seat to anchor her body. Slowly, she stood again, her back to the steering wheel and her eyes still fixed on the damaged end of the boat.

The once peaceful water now jerked in frantic waves around her, rocking the boat.

Confused and slightly disoriented, she managed to start the engine. She was just reaching the bay when the surface of the water rose high into the air and something big lunged toward her. She was shoved backward by an ostensibly invisible force, right into the ignition. Sharp pain pinched her upper back as she swallowed a mouthful of salt water. She tried coughing, but could only gag. Scrambling across the floor of the boat, she managed to open the compartment where she kept their KA-BAR, an Ek Model 4. Grasping it with both hands, she pushed herself up against the wall of the boat.

The unknown force became visible. Large, horned teeth came for her.

Rian slashed the side of its face.

Too late, she realized her left foot was dangling just over the edge of the boat. The sea monster, an enormous Great White, settled its huge mouth around her shoe and yanked on it. The shoe peeled off and she jerked her foot back inside before it could sink its teeth into her flesh.

Rian found her voice and screamed. Her scream was not a howl of pain, but one of terror.

***

Deep inside the water, its gigantic body sank farther away from the light of day and from the warmer temperature of the island, 4,000 feet downward inside the massive ocean. The bottom of the ocean was dark and fiercely cold. The crystal water massaged the shark's body as it restlessly swam. For a short while, the shark stayed at the bottom of the ocean. But only for a short while.

Chapter Two

It wasn't always this way. Rian at the top of her game with a husband and a career from dreams she'd only once been able to fantasize about. Here she was, thirty-five years old, with everything she'd worked so hard for. But now things were not looking so good for her. No, they were not looking so good at all.

She placed her hand over her heart, but she couldn't feel a pulse. Her shoulder shriveled downward as her body slid down the wall of the boat. She couldn't feel anything. Weakly, she glanced at the clock on the bow. Five o'clock. Jack wouldn't be home from work until midnight. Her fingers were shaking, slight erratic movements that reminded her.

She shut her eyes. The memory came at her.

They saw her before she saw them. From tangled gossamer-like shadows, two shadowy figures emerged from the crevice of the door. They seemed to blend with the night as though they were a part of it.

A skeleton face stood out in the black space of the doorframe.

Rian smiled. It was some kind of a Halloween prank. She took a step away from her car and moved toward the house.

Only this was November.

She stopped. Something was wrong. She spun on her heel, screamed, and lifted one leg in midair in an effort to run back to the car.

Too late.

A gloved hand clamped around her mouth, cutting off her scream, whirled her around, and shoved her toward the house. A second dark shape, the skeleton, hooked an elbow around her throat as the other figure pushed her down the narrow hallway. A full body mirror was glued on the wall at the end of the hall, but all she could see were the mysterious shapes looming over her, a white skeleton face and a black shapeless cloth covering the face of the other person.

The skeleton shouted at her. "On the ground!"

She landed on her keys and phone, desperate to hide them. With her face partially stuffed into the carpet, all she could see were two pairs of shoes moving back-and-forth between the bathroom that stood a few inches away and her face.

She jolted back from her memory. *Freedom* had anchored itself against the dock beside a few other boats. She looked up to see that the sun was gone so all that remained was a black sky. She had fallen asleep.

As she leapt out of the boat, Rian felt a hard jolt. She screamed as she jumped away from the water's edge. It was just the jerking motion of the boat. The water was now quietly lapping at the surface. Rian nervously scanned the water, her eyes quickly darting left to right, north to south. No shark.

The dock was wet as she sat down. Sliding a few yards away from the water, she found herself lying down, trying to catch her breath, her heart gasping out of shock, her arms twitching in fear.

Spaced every five yards, streetlamps faced the single lane of the harbor. A small handful of businesses lined the street, but all the windows were shrouded in darkness.

Rian frowned and looked down at her watch: 9:13. She had been passed out for over four hours. She glanced back at the swaying boat, noticing that the right side of the body had been punched inward.

This is it, Rian. The end of the road. You have completed your mission. It is time to go. They were thoughts from the past. When she had almost died.

And here she was again, though in a very different situation, still seconds away from death.

"Oh, God!" she started gasping, but all the air she took in

was too thick and it made her cough.

The black ocean looked bottomless. She shuddered and looked away.

The lamppost above her head burned into her eyes. She squinted as tears fired into her soul. She opened her mouth and a blast of cold air poured inside of it. Coughing again, she gradually rose, stepped forward, and stopped. Her heart felt heavy as it pressed down inside of her. The boardwalk stretched far. Too far.

Her body buckled beneath her.

"Rian? Rian!" The voice sounded so far away. She tried to open her eyes, but it was as if a strong weight pulled her eyelids back down. "Stay with us, Rian." The voice was urgent. "Don't move!"

A bright light stared down into her face; it came from the ceiling beams. She tried to move her arm, but it was too painful. She slowly turned her head to the left. A starch white wall faced her. To her right, a window opened into a view of a cemetery.

The clock on the nightstand read 7:00 a.m. On a rolling cart, next to her bed, an IV was feeding fluids into her left arm. No wonder she couldn't move it. She tried to sit up, but her breath caught in her chest and she quickly lied back down. Next to her head was a nurse-call button. She managed to move her right arm and punch the button. Within seconds, a nurse arrived. He carried himself with formality, but when he reached her bedside and smiled, Rian felt immediately comfortable.

"How are you feeling?" he asked.

She remembered Nurse Jon. When she'd first regained consciousness, it had been three in the morning. She had explained everything in detail about the shark attack. Clearly, the nature of the event had exhausted her for she had quickly fallen back asleep.

"You're doing much better, Rian, especially after your meeting with an unfriendly shark."

"You mean, there are friendly sharks out there?"

He smiled at her as he adjusted the tubes in her arm.

She recalled the night before and knew it would be a moment that would repeat the memory of itself for years. A dark gloomy shape opened its mouth for her—

"How's the pain?"

"When I try to move, it hurts."

"You lost a lot of blood."

"How long?"

"What's that?"

"When do I get to go home?"

"You're lucky. The shark didn't get a piece of you, but your body hit the wheel pretty hard. You received fifteen stitches in your head. You're going to be sore for a while—the impact from being pushed into the boat bruised your chest and back, but we should have you out of here tomorrow night."

She cringed as she remembered the darkness folding in all around her and how her breath nearly knocked out of her as her back slammed into the ignition.

"Where's my husband?"

"He just stepped out, but he will be back shortly. He went for some coffee." Nurse Jon dumped a capsule into his palm and held out a cup of water. "Tylenol for the pain." She eagerly accepted both and immediately swallowed the pill. "I'll be doing my rounds now, but if you need anything, just push the button."

Minutes later, Jack arrived. He carried a cup of steaming coffee in his hand, but he sat it down on the table against the wall. "Rian!" He rushed to her side. Even at the age of thirty-eight, he still had all of his hair, but he chose to keep his blond strands in a buzz cut. "Once a Marine, always a Marine". He retired in July from the Marine Corp, having served his twenty years in HMH-466 as a 6173 Helicopter Crew Chief on CH-53

Super Stallions.

"The nurse said I could go home tomorrow."

"Oh, Rian, thank God you're all right." He embraced her gently, careful to avoid the IV and the bruising in her chest. "What do you need? Are you hungry at all?"

She shook her head. "Did we win?"

Jack laughed. "Still got your priorities, I see. Nah, the Bengals won, but we'll get to the playoffs. It's a definite."

They chatted like that for the next several minutes and Rian started feeling a lot better, almost forgetting about the pain.

"Who found me?" she asked.

"What?"

"On the pier. Who found me? When?"

***

The shark detected movement about five hundred feet away. It glided swiftly through the water. Smaller sea life scrambled out of its way, fearful of its size, yet respectful of its power. Propelling itself forward, the massive fish pushed tirelessly toward the source. It navigated the waters about fifteen miles per hour as it closed in on its prey. The distance shortened. Now ten yards separated it from the moving object overhead. Five yards, three yards. WHACK! It smacked the side of the boat. Its fin barely surfaced as it pushed straight toward the humming motor it sensed above.

***

"Hal found you."

Hal Robertson, owner of *Hal's Sweets*, had been a good friend to them since their move here three years ago. His business was one of the earlier establishments on Balboa Island, located in between a dog boutique and bakery. She and

Jack had a Golden Retriever, Champ, who they took for walks beside the harbor, so the two side-by-side storefronts catered to them perfectly because all three of them had sweet teeth.

More like family than a friend, Hal welcomed the Fields into his life as if they had known each other for years. He'd lost his wife to cancer five years before, after spending thirty years of marriage together. Perhaps his loss is what caused him to take on a grandfatherly type role and treat Jack and Rian as if they were his own family. They had spent many evenings in his houseboat toasting Rian's new career and the renovation of the Southern California Marine Institute.

During his Marine Corp career, Jack did a lot of part time construction work on the side. Though a retired Gunnery Sergeant, he still found joy in helping local businesses. The Institute's Nimitz docks were in need of repair. Jack jumped at the chance yesterday and so had begun the first official planning meeting last night. Which also meant that next week she would be leading a day trip for student instruction. She needed to possess some sort of familiarity with the water, so Westen's decision made sense. And now she was familiar, *too* familiar.

"Why was a Great White so close to the island? Even those spotted three hundred yards from the peninsula are rarely seen," she said as she pushed herself up in bed.

Jack took her hand and shook his head.

"It was at least twenty feet long," she continued, her heart thudding. "I wasn't even looking for it. I was just relaxing, not working."

"How are you doing, sweetie?"

"Hal!"

He smiled and gently hugged her.

"We were really worried about you, kid. You gave us a good scare."

"The nurse said I should be able to go home tomorrow night."

"Good news."

"I've already let Lilah know," Jack told her.

Lilah was Rian's oldest and best friend. They had grown up together in Maryland. Lilah still lived there with her husband and two kids. They called each other every day and visited each other at least twice a year.

"Thank you." She kissed Jack.

The three of them talked for about an hour until Nurse Jon returned to let them know that she needed her rest.

"I'll be in touch soon. You just rest and get better, sweetie," Hal kissed her forehead and left.

Nurse Jon wrote some notes on his clipboard and dimmed the lights before exiting the room.

Rian pulled the blanket up under her chin, closing her eyes. And then the headache came. Torrents of rain poured into her skull and battered her with long clamps of steel. Nearly two years ago, that November, a headache hit her hard for the first time, just after the incident. It pounded her for days. But this one was far more excruciating, and with it came an unexpected sense of dread.

Chapter Three

Rian was released the next day as promised. Jack took her home to change and insisted that she take some time off. They would be meeting their small circle of friends for dinner at Bayside Restaurant, their favorite dining place near the island. Rian protested, but eventually gave in, agreeing that she could use some more company.

By the time they got to their table, the restaurant had filled up. Lively conversation brought a cheerful element to the atmosphere. An old Van Morrison song played over the speakers, barely audible above the happy noise.

They were all there, their closest friends here. The married couples, Dylan and Shonda, and Sean and Kristen, and the two single guys, Randy and Floyd. Rian was more than content to be around everyone for she was able to forget, at least for a little while, the events of the other day. And then a wonderful surprise walked through the door—Lilah and her husband, Luke.

***

He couldn't wait to reveal his secret. She had been on his mind for so long that it was becoming more difficult to keep the truth. He was worried that he would be found out. It wasn't guilt that he felt, of course, but the desire to return to her once more and have her relive that night was becoming harder to suppress. He needed to finish what had been started.

***

"Rian!" Lilah practically ran into her as Rian met her halfway.

Lilah, her oldest and best friend, was "the good girl". She grew up an only child and her parents had placed a lot of expectations on her that she had obediently met. Sometimes Rian saw her as an angel, too good for this world.

"I can't believe you're here. I mean, Jack didn't say anything."

"I know. We kept it a secret. It was very last minute. Rian, after he told me what happened, Luke and I agreed, we needed to come out here."

"We're always here for you, you know that." Luke hugged Rian. Luke was a suit-and-tie man that exuded success. He was always wearing a dark pair of sunglasses, which belied his preppy look and created an image of a "Mr. Cool".

"How are you today?" Lilah asked as they joined everyone at the table.

"OK, I guess. Lilah, it was the scariest. . .I thought I was going to die." She shivered at the memory. Lilah pressed her hand over Rian's and squeezed it.

Everybody ordered some type of seafood for their meal, except for Rian. She didn't like fish, neither the kind you ate nor the kind that ate you, so she settled on a 12 oz. steak, medium well. Just another quirk Jack poked fun of her for, a Marine Biologist who moved near an island, navigated sea life for a living, but didn't like the water or the taste of sea creatures.

Rian looked around at everyone, her body began to relax. She was fortunate to have each of these people in their lives. They had all been there for her that November two years ago. As she listened to their individual conversations, she took pleasure in just watching each of them.

Dylan was from Cuba. His family immigrated to the United States fifty years ago. He had served in the Marines with Jack and he carried a wit that matched no other. He was relatively young, twenty-five, so Rian was always telling him he should go into show business, but he always insisted that she was the only one who thought he was actually funny. Whenever she tried to convince him otherwise, that he really did have a gift for making people laugh, he would only laugh in reply.

Dylan's wife, Shonda, worked with Rian at the Institute. While Rian had a pale complexion, strawberry blond hair, and stood about 5'10, Shonda looked the complete opposite. She was petite, about 5'2, a dark-haired Asian beauty with a self-confidence that was refreshingly humble. More often than not, she was at work on one project or another at the Institute.

Sean had also served in the Marines with Jack. Actually, Jack had met him through Dylan and the three of them quickly formed a close bond. Sean was about a foot taller than Shonda. He was quiet for the most part and polite. But his wife, Kristen, was the life of the party.

A bright charismatic red-head, Kristen exuded an energy that made Rian feel a special joy for life. Whenever she was feeling down, Kristen's presence lifted her. Kristen and Sean were complete opposites, but their relationship was perfect.

She and Jack met Randy at this very restaurant. His dark shoulders were covered in tattoos—sketches of dragons mostly, and the initials of his ex-girlfriend—those he regretted. He had the face of a sun bronzed angel, but a quick-tempered nature. Just above his left eye was a small slash, a scar from his troubled past. He and a guy fought over some girl years ago, but he'd grown up since then.

Randy was almost forty and had been their server one night. Turned out that he and Rian had a lot in common. He also graduated from UMBC and came out here after his longtime girlfriend broke up with him. He'd been heartbroken and needed a change in geography. He had family out here and moved in with his cousin while he got back on his feet. Rian had spoken to her supervisors and they hired Randy on the spot for an internship.

Floyd was the oldest of the group, forty-two, and a very eligible bachelor. He was a model type, tall, thin, dark skin, spell-binding eyes. A smooth talker, he kept the energy of the group going like an unbreakable tape that kept them all together. Whenever any one of them was down or if there was ever tension between them, he would be there to ensure that peace was made. He was the harmonizer of the group. And he worked as a freelance editor for various publishers.

When the food came, they quieted down, just enjoying the rich taste of their meals. The atmosphere proved light, easy, for some time, and the horror of the shark attack lost its grip on Rian momentarily. Being in the company of their friends brought her reassurance that she was still alive, that death could be abated awhile. She looked around at everyone and thought, this is the life, simple but good.

Then Sean excused himself from the table. When he returned a moment later, there was a strange look on his face. "There's been an accident. Some locals were killed earlier today by a Great White. They were just showing it on the news," he said softly.

"Is it the one?" Jack asked. Rian's body tensed. *Please let it be.*

He acted reluctant, nervous. "They are still investigating, but there was another accident, late last night, and they are pretty sure it's that shark. Not sure if it's," he looked at Rian, "your shark."

"I'm sure we'll know something soon," Lilah smiled.

Rian nodded. But she didn't feel so sure that the shark would match the one who had tried to get her. She pushed her dinner away.

Lilah cupped her hand over Rian's. Her fingers trembled underneath her friend's hand.

"Don't worry. We'll know soon enough." Lilah was trying to be reassuring, but Rian knew something was very wrong about all of this. It wasn't just about the shark. Something else was bothering her, but she didn't know what it was. And attempting to explain herself at that moment would only make her sound confused. So she said nothing.

Jack draped her coat over her shoulders and helped her up. "Come on, let's get home. After you get some sleep, you'll feel better."

Randy gave her a quick hug. "It's going to be OK." She nodded at him and mouthed a thank you to Lilah as Jack escorted them outside. As she pressed her hand to the restaurant's door, she noticed her fingers shaking and she wondered why the news had reawakened such fear in her.

Outside in the cooling evening, leaves fell through the air like rain. Some swirled and triple-spun while others rocked from side to side as they gradually descended to the ground. Yet, in the crisp night air, Rian felt strangely exposed to the world.

When they got home, she sank into the couch while her wonderful and thoughtful husband brought her a mug of black coffee. They had been married ten years. She wished she had found him sooner. Instead, she spent more than a decade going from one bad relationship to another. But when she met Jack, all that changed.

He had grown up in Maryland, too, and was visiting his parents one summer when he ran into Rian, literally. She was on her way to a book shop in Baltimore's Inner Harbor, minding her own business, when he came out of the store and smacked his shoulder into her neck. It was an awkward way to meet, to say the least. He'd apologized profusely. He'd had his nose in a book and had been so consumed by what he was reading that he hadn't even realized he'd stepped out of the bookstore.

Rian didn't fall for him at first. She'd been too busy rubbing at the bruise on her neck to notice that he'd slipped away to get her a cup of coffee and a single-stemmed pink carnation by way of apology. Before she'd taken either from him, she'd insisted on seeing his reading material.

"I need to know what was so intriguing that you couldn't see anything around you."

He immediately pulled out the hardback to show her. And that's when she fell for him. It was a copy of Stephen King's *Misery*. King was her all-time favorite author, but she had never met anyone who liked him as much as she did.

Months later, Jack's family met with hers and weeks after that, they had a grand ceremony at Fells Point. The weather had been excellent—a tinted sun and a soothing breeze— as they exchanged vows. Lilah and Luke had recently married and they willingly filled the roles of Matron of Honor and Best Man for their best friends. Because Jack was recently stationed in California, they'd agreed to a honeymoon in town for the week. They spent the second week packing her things and saying goodbye to Lilah and Luke, Rian's parents, and Jack's. And now, here they were.

"I'm sorry about the boat."

"The boat?"

"You told me to come watch you work. I should have."

He turned to look at her, his sea-green eyes gentle and magnetizing. "You will not blame yourself for this. I refuse to let you."

But Rian didn't feel any better. Jack had mistaken her words for a feeling of guilt. But she wasn't upset about the incident. She was upset that she had been alone. Vulnerable. Just like that night two years ago. She was just beginning to clarify that, when her cell phone rang.

"I'll get it." He went into the kitchen. She heard a muffled voice, but wasn't sure who it was.

She took a sip of the hot coffee and it tingled against her lips. Closing her eyes, she let her head slowly fall back into the cushion, and her hand relaxed. Jack was right. As soon as she got some rest, she would feel a lot better.

She heard Jack's voice as if it were coming not from the kitchen but from the end of the hall. "No, she's fine. I'm sure. . .Yeah, I'll be sure she takes some time off. . .right, a few days."

She opened her eyes and saw a blurry Jack coming back into the living room. "Who was that?"

He sank down next to her. "Randy. It was kind of, uh, interesting."

"What do you mean?"

"I don't know. He's not usually so pushy, but he insisted I make sure that you get rest."

Rian laughed. "My big brother."

"Yea, I guess." Jack smiled at her, but in his eyes she could see he wasn't assured.

"Hey," she reached over to touch his face. "I will be OK. Just take me to bed." His eyes sparkled with hope. "For sleep, Jack." He feigned disappointment.

When her head hit the pillow, the last thing she remembered hearing was Jack's voice in the doorway. "I'm going to watch some TV. I'll join you in about an hour."

Chapter Four

"When I lie down I say,
'When shall I arise?' But the night continues
And I am continually tossing until dawn" Job 7:4

She was in the ocean, but not on a boat. She was swimming this time, without a mask or swim gear of any kind. She had been holding her breath for several minutes and the pressure in her ears had become unbearable. Blood poured into her skull and a blackness started to smear her vision, her head filled with physical agony.

A baby was tumbling near some coral reef and blood was pouring out of the baby's heart. The pounding stopped inside her skull. A thin ribbon of blood trailed from her head and into the baby's heart.

A shark suddenly appeared, like the one Rian saw in real life. It closed in on them fast, coming right at them with a ferocious craving that had been waiting too long.

She woke up and stared at Jack who was asleep, his leg dangling off the side of the bed, his mouth slightly open, the way he had probably slept since he was a child. She loved this man so much and couldn't imagine life without him. She touched the side of his face.

"Hey," she gently whispered. "It's after noon." He moaned and blinked several times, trying to wake up. He looked at her through those pearl green eyes and her heart jumped even after all these years. "Let's go for a walk," she told him. "We've been working so hard. It's time for a break."

They decided on Balboa Island. They enjoyed strolling the island because it was sometimes pleasurable to get lost in the crowds. And it was pleasantly mind-numbing to take in all the places of business. Jane's Corn Dogs, Azar's Pizza, the Arcade, and the Market, among numerous other establishments.

For a nice, warm Saturday afternoon, not many people were strolling Balboa Island's walkway. For some reason, Rian felt safer, but she couldn't understand why. Normally, she enjoyed being in crowds. Separating them from the bay, where the Sundancer was normally docked, was the auto ferry fronted by ocean-front homes.

As they passed the section of water, she glanced behind her to that place of adversity. The shark was probably long gone. The ocean looked serene as miniature waves skipped over its glossy surface. Nevertheless, she shivered.

As she and Jack walked hand in hand, it occurred to her that she hadn't actually talked to him about the shark attack. The doctor and nurses held all the details and she assumed they discussed them with Jack, but she and Jack hadn't said much about any of it.

"Jack?" She stopped and turned to look at him. Rian wanted to tell him everything, just let the whole crazy story spill out until every last word and every fearful emotion expelled from inside her. Maybe then if she shared everything with Jack, she'd find relief from this disquieting feeling. "We haven't talked about what happened."

"What do you want to talk about?"

"Just the details of it. I've been feeling weird. I think that if I talk about it, like everything about it, with you, that maybe I'll be able to shake this. . .this uneasiness."

Jack pulled her toward a bench in front of Hal's storefront and waited for her to begin. She started from the point where she was feeling so good about their lives here, how much they had accomplished already, and thinking how promising their futures would be. But then how quickly she began to feel entirely alone out there when something slammed with full force into the boat. "It was like an earthquake tore into me. I thought I heard my skull crack as it hit the steering wheel. And without warning a roar came, a cry so loud and intent on getting to me." She stopped and once more her hands began to twitch as they had the other night. Jack grabbed them and held them closely to his chest.

"We can talk more later."

"No. I need to do this."

He nodded and waited for her to continue.

"Something warm was dripping down my face. It was my own blood. Before I could react, the monster smashed into the boat again and a rush of water poured onto the floor of the boat. I was thrown into the steering wheel a second time, and I swear I could feel a bruise forming. The shark was like an invisible force. I couldn't even see it the whole time. Not until the very end."

Jack held her for several minutes. He kissed her forehead, her lips. "We'll get through this," he told her.

They joined hands again and got up from the bench. Seagulls cried as they soared overhead. Waves whispered as they kicked up tiny grains of sand. But something plagued her.

Monster. Why had she called it a monster? Many people may have used the synonym for such a fish, so it wasn't that eccentric of a word choice, but something about it took on a special hidden meaning that eluded her.

In front of them, a small number of people came in and out of the many establishments that ornamented the walkway. *Hal's Sweets* stood out to her more than the others. The bright pink lettering over the doorframe blinked the store's name in glittering lights. Her heart warmed at the sight, and she forgot for the moment about the incident.

Hal winked at them as they walked through the door. A couple were trying to determine whether or not to get chocolate covered strawberries or chocolate covered cherries while their toddler girls grabbed peppermint sticks from the candy jar.

Rian glanced down at her hands. They were shaking more visibly now. But why?

"Hey, kids!" Hal winked at them as they came up to the counter. He was always calling them kids, his term of endearment for them. He and Shirley had been unable to have children. So while there was playfulness in his greeting, his affectionate pet name for them was more of a need than a game of fun. Hal and Shirley experienced an amazing love that most people never did or took the chance to, a kind of love that endured regardless of any situation, a love strong enough to endure the pain of seven miscarriages.

Rian stepped behind the counter to kiss Hal's cheek. He grabbed her and Jack and pulled them into a bear hug before letting them go. "Where's Champ?"

"He's catching up on the latest soaps," Jack said.

"Tell him he'd better come see me soon or I'm going to set him up on another date with that dreadful poodle." They all laughed. "So, what will it be today? Dark or milk?"

"My heart's a bit down. I think some dark will do it good," Rian told him. She pinned a smile to her lips, but both men knew her too well. Jack squeezed her hand and Hal's eyes teared up. A moment later he came out with a silver tray of dark chocolate covered strawberries.

"Any news?" Hal asked. They both shook their heads no.

"What is it?" Jack looked at her. He hadn't been fooled. Something more was going on here, and he knew it.

Rian bit into a strawberry, relishing the sweet taste before she began. "I don't know how to explain it. When I'm around people I sense that something's wrong. Or that someone is nearby." Her hands started shaking again and she tried hiding them under the tray but that only created an obvious tinny sound. "I hate this. Just like what I went through before. . .I can't go through that again."

"Sweetheart, we're going to see you through this. We'll help figure out what's bothering you. That's a promise better than the taste of my chocolates." Hal winked.

"Thank you, Hal."

"Rian." Jack set the tray on the counter and took her hands in his. "You said it felt like someone was nearby. What did you mean by 'someone'?"

"I feel like I'm in danger."

"When did you feel this?"

"Just now on the pier."

Hal nodded. "That makes sense. This is right where the shark attack happened."

"But I'm not thinking of that. It's something else. Someone." She groaned and rubbed away the tears that were spilling steadily down her cheeks now. Jack caressed her face. He took a strawberry off the plate and fed it to her while Hal filled two glasses with iced water.

Being in such close proximity to that terrible night was bound to evoke such feelings of distress. Revisiting places of great trauma often sparked the stress associated with them. But she remembered the restaurant and the same feeling of dread, of something terribly wrong enveloping her even there.

"No!" They both looked up. "It wasn't just now. It happened at the restaurant too. Remember when Sean gave us the news about the shark attack? I started feeling it then that something wasn't right. I don't know what it was, just that I was certain about it. Just like. . ." she glanced out the front window and into the lapping waves. "Just like I did out there."

They both remained quiet, neither one knowing what to say. Her mind was on the nightmare. The bloody baby and the shark coming after them so fast. What did it mean? She wanted to tell them, but she had to make sense of it first or it would just come out sounding like a baffling mess.

Sometimes Rian missed living more isolated. They spent the first seven years of their marriage in a quaint cottage home in a rural neighborhood. She knew it made sense to move here considering her career track, but her heart continued to ache for that sense of remote living. Now they lived in a place that was close enough to Hollywood to be inspired by the dream of fame but just far enough away to remain untainted by its false promise of true happiness.

The three of them stepped outside, spending the next hour with simple talk. Dark, cumulus-shaped clouds drifted slowly by. The sun had set in the western horizon, leaving behind a faint orange trail. Quickly, the clouds passed over the sun's footprints, soaping themselves in its oily color. Lightning flickered, illuminating the dark blue heavens. An instant later, thunder crackled. Car alarms went off and people shouted in excitement as they scattered in various directions, seeking refuge from the coming downpour.

Rian stood on the pier as a laundry of noises fell on all sides of her. The thought in her mind was a dangerous one. Dangerous because she didn't fully understand it totally just yet, and dangerous because, and she didn't quite know where this thought was coming from nor why she was so certain of it, she was in danger.

"You OK?" Jack put his arm around her, and she jumped slightly.

"Sorry."

"Don't apologize."

As they said their goodbyes to Hal, she tried not to worry.

They lived in a gated community of Bonita Canyon, a neighborhood in Newport Beach, close to Balboa Island. Recently remodeled, their home featured many upgrades that the original owner felt inspired to add in later years. Acacia hardwood flooring spanned most of the house. The kitchen included the most impressive appliances replete with marble counter tops and a chef's island.

The master suite included its own fireplace where she and Jack spent many nights getting ready for bed. The spacious backyard held a stainless steel BBQ grill, Jacuzzi, and its own casita where a guest could feel like he had his own getaway.

To Rian, their home symbolized the light at the end of the tunnel. For most of her life, she struggled paycheck to paycheck, stressing over paying school loans and finding consistent work. After so many years, her life was going in a better direction. Gone were the financial constraints that once prevented her from finding success. But not just in the monetary sense. Being with Jack, finding her niche in the marine biology world and the amazing close-knit circle of friends was better than anything money could ever buy, and right now, more than ever, she couldn't have wished for anything better. Which was why she was disturbed by the insistent nudging that her life was in jeopardy.

Jack turned on a classic rock station and for the short ride home, they rode in silence, holding each other's hands. She glanced out the window at the passing streetlights and sighed. She looked forward to sinking into bed and forgetting about the suspicions that had overtaken her.

Champ greeted them at the door, his golden paws attacking them before they could get a word out. He whimpered with joy, his tail wagging, as he nudged them with his nose.

Rian said, "Missed us, huh, boy? Don't worry. We'll be sure to take you with us to Hal's next time. He asked about you."

The dog's ears arched and he barked softly as if he understood. She laughed and scratched behind Champ's ears. "Wanna treat?"

Rian pulled out a rawhide stick from behind her back. He immediately sat, his brown eyes wide, but patient, as he obediently awaited the delicious savor of the meat. She tossed it in his mouth and he gratefully accepted it as he padded off down the hall.

They decided to catch up on some of their favorite TV shows, but Rian quickly grew tired. It was nearing midnight, and though she had never been much of a nocturnal owl anyway, she wondered why she felt more tired than usual. She supposed the last few days had really gotten to her, not only mentally, but physically as well. A nice long sleep, she hoped, would rejuvenate her. Jack joined her in the bedroom.

As she passed the window, she had this sudden irrational thought that someone would start spraying bullets through it. The certainty was so powerful that she stepped quickly past the window and to her dresser where she stood frozen for a few seconds. It wasn't the first time she'd felt this way. Even though the threat to her life had taken place two years before, the reminder of it, it seemed, would never cease. That she had been attacked by a shark hadn't helped either. Was that why she was experiencing this anxiety again?

Jack looked over at her as he changed into his boxers, knowing what the rigidity of her body meant, knowing her so well. "You're anxious because of that night. But we're OK, Rian. Trust me."

That's what she wanted more than anything, to trust in his words.

She dressed in her warm pajamas, slid beneath the covers, and fixed her eyes upon the window. Waiting. A minute passed and she continued to lie there very still, her body stiff with anticipation, her eyes locked on the thin pane of glass that separated her from potential danger.

Just after Jack kissed her goodnight, she fell asleep and relived more of that night.

Night came in the form of an ominous shadow. Black satin paint covered the entire span of the sky, hiding the stars. The moon was nowhere to be found. All light ceased on that cold November evening. It was Black Friday, November 29th, but the nightfall welcomed only the bleakest of things, the most gloomy, and only the very darkest of thoughts and dreams.

Wind blew across the trees, a hollow tunnel-like shriek. Rian sat in her car, enjoying the heat from the vents. She noticed the porch light was off, which she thought was strange as Jack always made sure to leave it on when he was home. But then she remembered. He had called her at the bar to say he wouldn't be home for another three hours. They enjoyed a brief simple conversation. Just an hour ago she had been full of happiness. But now something had changed.

She glanced outside again, at the forbidden night. A film of frost covered the windshield and she rubbed at the window with the palm of her hand feeling the coolness against her skin. When she pulled her hand away, she was startled to see icy particles sprinkled across the tips of her fingers. How could that be? It seemed that even the cold found its way inside her. Like it was looking for her.

She shivered, not so much from the cold touch of the frost but from something within.

The rearview mirror reflected part of her face. She switched on the overhead light and stared into it. Her entire life she'd been told that she was a pretty girl. But she had never been called beautiful. The black opal Jack had given her on their first anniversary hung from a thick silver chain around her neck. The iridescent gem surrounded by diamonds, Jack would tell her, complemented her dark brown eyes. But her nose was too big and her cheeks too round. She had always liked her body, but she could have done without her face. A small brown mole, in the shape of a perfect circle, met the corner of her lip. She had been told by many people that because of that mole she'd make a great model.

She had delivered pizzas and waitressed instead.

The front door remained shrouded in shadows. Her heart shook a little. Rian Field had never been afraid of anything in her life. Even when her father passed away three years ago, she had not shed a single tear. His death hadn't scared her. It had only made her stronger. She was a firm believer in living life to the fullest because, as she quickly discovered after he passed away, life lasted for such a short time. It seemed

31

ridiculous to Rian to spend too much time worrying over things. Besides, once you died, that was it. No more pain. No more sorrow. No more worry.

She shook her head. She was alive. Alive! Why think such gloomy thoughts? She and Jack were in a really good place with a brand new home and her dream job. She hadn't even thought about her father's death in months.

Something wet fell from her blouse. She touched her forehead. It was damp.

The vents were blowing at full blast. She lowered the setting, switched off the ignition, grabbed her phone, and headed to the entry way. The front door swung open. Somebody grabbed her.

The first guy shoved her head into the wall. He commanded her to get on her stomach. The second guy told her to lift up and they grabbed the phone she had tried to hide underneath her. The keys made a tinkling sound as they yanked them from her grip. Before she could react, she was jerked up off the floor.

"Who are you? What are you doing here?!" A deep male voice demanded.

She blinked and blinked, but everything remained dark. The hall light had been shut off and her eyes were slowly adjusting to the shifting shadows that floated back and forth around her.

"What's your name?"

"Rian. Rian Field."

She jerked awake from the dream. Next to her, Jack softly snored.

Panic surrounded her in the stillness of the bedroom, her body violently trembling, her breath suspended. She let out a lungful of air, but it was shaky and it matched the hard rigid knocking of her heart. Like a wild river, the fear thrashed through her veins, attacking everything inside her. She squeezed her eyes shut so tightly that the muscles crushed up against the bones of her face.

Then the rest of the dream came to her.

Pain whooshed through her lungs, taking the very breath from them until she fell to her knees in the struggle to breathe. She wanted to scream, but the air was too dense in her diaphragm and no sound could escape her. Then, silence. Something brighter than the sun shined down on top of her head. She looked up from her place on the ground and squinted to see a hand reaching out for her.

Her breathing returned in soft strokes. The pain that had coursed its way fiercely through her entire body faded.

The ceiling fan above her rotated slowly, sending down a cool draft of air across her face. Her heart rose from the bleak sensations of the dream. From the memory. Why was she remembering it all over again? It had been two years since it had happened to her.

"Rian?" Jack sat up next to her. "What are you doing?"

"I had a nightmare. About that night."

"But what are you doing?" He nodded toward her hands.

She looked down and saw that she was embracing her stomach, her fists cupping the area in a protective embrace. "I. I don't know."

Jack detected the confusion and terror in her voice and he took her hands in his and pulled her close to him. His body was so warm and welcoming to her, and she leaned into him, closing her eyes, her tired, achy eyes.

Chapter Five

~November 7 2015~

The end of Autumn proved to be more vibrant than usual. Leaves of all colors held tenaciously to the trees until, finally, they could not resist their inevitable fall to earth. The golden foliage crunched under Rian's steps, a rainbow carpet of ruby-red, deep purple, chocolate, and neon-yellow. A soft breeze stirred the quiet air and embraced her like a coat.

She adored days like these with a lone walk in the park. In such solitude, she could almost believe that the world was made just for her. But soon things changed.

Dark charcoal clouds drifted overhead glaring down at her as if prophesying something formidable. The soft breeze suddenly converted into a gusty wind, picking up the leaves from the ground and blowing them east, some of them tearing and chipping from the wind's tenacious grip. The wind snapped weak limbs off of tree while bright-colored leaves were yanked from their branches and flung into the air, whipping and tossing frantically through the bitter-chilled air.

Rian huddled deeper inside her cotton sweatshirt, peeping through the tornado of twigs and debris that spun chaotically in her face. Jack was at work. She usually brought Champ along when Jack couldn't join her on these walks, but she decided to stroll alone to gather her thoughts about the dream, the memories.

She arrived at the center of the park and shivered as she looked around at what usually appeared harmless and normal, but now seemed somehow threatening. She rushed past the swings that swayed as if occupied by ghosts. Past the long curving slide that beckoned to her. Past the rows of gardenias, impatiens, and roses, running faster, harder, and the wind growing stronger as if propelling her forward of its own might. She pumped her legs more vigorously, desperate to reach the outskirts of the grounds. When she arrived at the edge of the park, she felt safe again, though she didn't know why, and she stopped to brush twigs and broken leaves from her sweater.

The charcoal clouds continued to move rapidly overhead, prematurely bringing in the night. They buried the red-purple sky and burned out the lights of heaven. And all of a sudden she knew that the dream was not just a flashback of that November night, but a premonition. She hurried to the car.

Searching for a distraction, she quickly switched on the stereo. Christmas was only weeks away and she was pleased to hear Elvis singing about a blue Christmas. As the steering wheel spun beneath her hands, her body began to relax and the bitter chill of the wind replaced by the warmth of the heater. Evidently, she left the park just in time.

Large flat drops of rain splattered against the windshield, snapping against it much like the sound of matches being struck across a matchbox. Rushing down in sheets, the rain closed tightly around the car like a beaded curtain.

Her pleasant mood quickly changed. Strangely, she felt trapped, not by the rain, but as if by someone. It was that same sensation on the boardwalk the other night when she and Jack visited Hal.

In a split second, the whole world fell backward into the night. The white glare of lightning burned into her eyes. Thunder snapped, pounding angrily behind the car. Too close.

She picked up her cell phone and punched in Jack's number. She couldn't control the shakiness in her voice as she begged him to come home. He was on break with Floyd; they were both on their way.

Inside their home, Rian began to feel secure again. Champ greeted her with a warm, wet tongue. She reached down to tug at his floppy ears, thankful for the simple pleasures of life.

Jack entered the kitchen carrying two bottles of Corona for Floyd and him and a glass of water for Rian. She held the cold glass to her lips. As if he suspected something was very wrong, Champ nudged her with his nose. He knew it wasn't typical for her to come home in such a lethargic condition.

"Remember our walk to see Hal, how it felt like something, no, *someone* was there?"

"Yes, baby," Jack held her hand. She stopped. How could she explain this? It was more like a feeling of terror, but just a feeling, without any explanation. Instead, she let her mind wander back to the shark.

"What in the world is a shark doing in those waters, I mean, in the bay? It doesn't belong there," she asked them both.

"Well, no, not typically," Floyd said. "But I'm sure there has to be an explanation. The ocean currents are always manipulating the atmosphere. So why not the other way around? With these constant changes in climate, the ocean's currents are surely impacted, which could influence the movement of sea life."

They both stopped sipping their drinks to stare at Floyd. "When did you get your PhD in climate and currents?" Jack joked. On a more serious note, he turned to Rian, brushing her hair away from her face. "We'll find out, baby, even if it takes a whole team of scientists."

She smiled, but inside she didn't believe that this situation could be simply reasoned. Not even the most educated of deep-sea divers or teams of scientists would be able to discover a logical explanation for what had happened to her. They may explain how the shark managed to wander into the bay, but they would not be able to explain why it had come after *her*.

Jack and Floyd started up a different conversation, but she hardly listened. Looking across at the living room, she found herself drawing closer to a state of normalcy. The TV Guide on the coffee table reminding her of the daily ritual. The oak entertainment center with its home-sweet-home charm. The framed photos of her and Jack, of their relatives, of friends gleaming brightly. All of it was comforting, familiar. She hoped it would last a while.

A few hours later, as it was nearing dusk, the phone rang. Rian jumped up to get it. It was Lilah. She and Luke were coming over for one last visit before they headed back east. Floyd decided to leave almost as soon as they arrived, but Rian was glad to spend some alone time with her oldest friends, just the four of them.

"Have they reported any news?" Luke asked about the shark. He removed his shades and she got a rare look at his crystalline eyes.

Rian shook her head. "We'll be lucky to ever see it again. It wasn't even supposed to be there." She stopped herself, shuddering inside. Wasn't supposed to be there. Like those masked men weren't supposed to be there when she arrived home. She knew that the two events were so utterly different from one another, so why did she feel like this similarity was significant, like something that was linking them together?

"Honey, what is it?" Lilah was the first to speak. But how could she begin to tell them? What could she say? That a shark attack reminded her of that November night? Jack would just urge her back into therapy. No. She didn't want to go back. She had made too much progress already. And yet, the nightmares had returned too. She had yet to tell anyone because she was hoping they would go away, but the eerie quality of them too closely reflected the reality from two years before. Though that didn't really make much sense as the incident and the content of the dream were vastly different from each other. So, why did it seem like they were connected?

"Rian." Jack's eyes, ever-changing, were now a soft pearl

turquoise, as he stared at her with concern. "Are you OK?"

"No. No, I'm not." She looked around at them, one at a time, and hoped that when she spoke her next words, she wouldn't feel alone in this dark haze.

"Whatever it is, we will all go through it with you." Lilah gently took her friend's hands in hers to encourage her to go on. Rian smiled at her, but she felt more pain than happiness.

"I've been having the nightmares again. They take me through the beginning of that night and it's just like before, where I can't see who they are and everything, the room, the hallway, they're too dark. Each time I dream about it, a little bit more happens. I don't know how to explain it except it's something like putting together a really difficult puzzle and I'm just starting to figure out where the middle pieces go." She took a deep breath and closed her eyes.

They waited for her patiently, Lilah squeezing her hands, Jack's fingers nestling against her cheek, Luke faintly smiling at her from his place next to Lilah. "I had a different dream the other night. I was deep in the ocean and I saw a baby floating around. I know it's because of the miscarriage, I'm sure that's what it is." Lilah took her hand and squeezed. "But then there was a shark. . .no, *the* shark, and it started to come at us." She glanced at each of them and they looked at her expectantly, patiently, with eyes of compassion. How grateful she was to have these people in her life. Would they be able to help her, especially when she said what she did next? "But I think these are the same dreams."

"Like they're somehow related?" Lilah asked, looking more concerned than confused. Good old Lilah, always so perceptive, even when Rian didn't want her to be. Luke and Jack exchanged looks, not quite sure what to make of her statement.

"I know they don't sound like they have any connection, but there's something about them, I guess the way they make me feel so that they seem intertwined somehow." And somehow they are like the real event two Novembers ago.

Lilah nodded. "In both dreams, you are in danger. You're scared."

"Right. But I don't think that's all they have in common." They looked at her, waiting for an explanation. But she didn't have one.

Luke got up and whispered to Lilah. To Jack and Rian, she said, "We're going to get some carry out. Still like it Hawaiian style?" she asked them both. Her way of giving them space. She knew that Rian needed time to sort this out with Jack. Alone.

"Sounds good." Jack smiled. Once they left, he turned to Rian and said something that took her aback. "Let's move."

"What?" She was more than startled by his words. "No. Why?"

"You haven't been the same. Things started getting better, but now with these nightmares again and the shark attack, you being frightened at almost every step. It's this house, where that awful night happened. We have to leave. It's too close to the memory."

"No, that's ridiculous. This house is ours. We worked too hard for it." She backed away from him, feeling suddenly threatened.

Though Jack looked at her with a smile, in it was sorrow. "I know. Believe me, I know. But I have to take care of you." He picked up her hand and kissed it. "If we stay here, I won't be able to live with myself, watching you fall apart. You can't feel safe here. We tried. We tried so hard, but it's too unforgettable."

"Stop!" She jerked her hand away. He was stunned. She regretted hurting him, but she also felt adamant about staying. She left the room and practically ran down the hall to their bedroom.

Her mind was stirring up with an assortment of thoughts, fueled by anxiety and agony and turmoil. Why did she think these dreams were connected? How could they possibly be? Why had she gotten so angry with Jack? Why did she feel like her life was in danger, now more than ever? There were too many questions without any answers.

She entered their bedroom, collapsed on the bed face-first, and fell apart.

Jack knew her too well and he left her alone in the bedroom. Moments later came the sound of their friends and the smell of pepperoni and pineapple pizza. She wanted to join them and laugh and talk and forget about everything.

But what had happened couldn't be forgotten. No one except Rian truly knew the physical sensations of the pain and eeriness they inflicted on her that November night in 2013. She didn't need to think about it. It would do nothing but bring more pain.

Our Father, who art in heaven.

She sat up and held her breath. Where had that prayer come from? She didn't pray.

She looked around the room as if she might find the answer there. It got so quiet, just a little too quiet. Her heartbeat shot up into her throat and it was like those gloved hands were grabbing at her throat all over again. She started panting and clutching at the sheet. Something wet rolled inside her hand. She opened her palm and watched as a tiny ball of liquid dripped onto the teal-colored sheet. She touched her forehead—it was only sweat.

Her hands went to her neck, certain she would find the gloved fingers flexing against it. But nothing was there. Eyes closed, hands clasped, she drew in a deep breath and slowly let it out.

She rose from the bed and went to take a step toward the door but faltered. Losing equilibrium, she nearly tumbled into the dresser, but found her balance again and entered the living room.

Lilah turned in her seat and smiled, holding out a plate

with two bubbling pieces of pizza. "Eat up, friend!"

Jack tried not to show his worry as he pasted a smile on his face. He kissed Rian's cheek and opened a can of Pepsi for her.

"Hey, Rian. We're glad we were able to make it out. Sorry we have to leave so soon, but work calls." Luke spoke between bites.

"Of course. I live that story too," Rian responded. They all shared a small laugh and spent the next several minutes eating in silence. Nothing would change the way she felt. They all knew that to be true.

She was really going to miss Lilah. She wished there was some way of keeping her here, but without over concerning them she really had no sensible way of doing it. The last thing she wanted to be was a burden.

When it was time for them to leave, Lilah held her close, like she knew how much pain she was in. "I'm right here," she said, tapping Rian's chest. "In your heart, wherever we are." It was a line she'd spoken to Rian years ago when she and Jack first moved away.

"Please call me every day if you can." Rian's inner insecurity betrayed her, but she didn't care.

"Absolutely." Lilah grinned and hugged her.

"We'll plan another trip soon." Luke promised as he shook Jack's hand and hugged Rian.

Her heart sank a little as she watched them go. Jack came up beside her and took her in his arms. His scratchy unshaven chin gently rubbed against the side of her cheek, so real and protecting.

Jack spoke up a minute later. "Floyd called earlier, and he's coming back over, if that's all right with you. I told him to bring Randy along, but he said Randy couldn't make it."

She sniffed and wiped away some of the wetness around her eyes. "I'd like that."

Jack cupped her face between his hands. "I know how

41

much you'll miss Lilah, but I'll try to keep you from hurting too much." She started crying again, though this time the tears sprang from her thankful heart.

Champ padded into the room and stopped beside them. He cocked his head as if to ask what was wrong. Rian chuckled and rubbed his head. "We'll be all right, boy."

But when Floyd arrived later, he brought unexpected news. "There's been another shark attack. A teenaged boy this time. The fish sank its teeth into his side, a flesh wound. He's going to make it, but because of the frequency and the close proximity to the area where you were attacked, they suspect this may be the same shark that attacked you. The mayor is asking the two latest surviving victims to come forward."

"What for?" Jack asked.

"They want to examine the boy's wounds." He faced Rian. "And they want to take a look at the boat damage."

"*Freedom*? Why? How is that supposed to help?" she asked.

"The Mayor believes that there may be a way to connect the boy's wounds with the damage the shark did to the boat. He's already hired a Marine Biologist to handle the diagnosis."

"Are you kidding me? I'm a Marine Biologist, for crying out loud."

Floyd pressed his lips together as if hesitant to proceed. "I know, Rian. He knows that, but he feels, and so does the chief of police and the news, that you are just too close to this. . ."

"To be objective," she finished and walked over to the bar. She poured herself a shot of tequila and downed it in a second. It burned a little because she wasn't used to it. She wasn't a drinker.

Jack was looking at her with sorrow in his face. He looked helpless, like he didn't know what to do. She rejoined them a few minutes later.

"So what happens next?" she asked Floyd.

"What do you mean?"

She was getting annoyed with the whole situation and impatient with Floyd. "When am I expected to meet up with them?"

"I don't know, Rian."

Her impatience gave way to anger. "Who are you to bring this news to me anyway? What gives you the right?" She moved closer to him until her face was inches away from his. He held up his hands and tried to put them on her shoulders, but she tore away from him. "Get out!"

"Rian!" Jack never shouted at her, and his tone surprised her. It was full of disappointment and reprimand. But they weren't going to treat her like a child. No one was going to tell her what to do.

"No, no, it's OK, Jack." Floyd held up his hands again as if in surrender. He threw his jacket over his arm as he went to the door. "I'm sorry, Rian. It's just what I saw on the news. I'll talk to you later." Before they could respond he closed the door.

Jack was looking at her in silence when she turned around. There was a real sadness in his eyes, like he had lost her. It couldn't be helped, she supposed. She hadn't meant to pull away from him earlier or snap at Floyd. She was sorry about all of it, but she was angrier than sorry and she went back to the bedroom without saying another word.

Chapter Six

"What was that all about?" Jack stepped into the room and he looked at her with what she thought to be pity.

Rian turned away. She refused to let herself get angry again. If she put her mind to it, she could control her emotions and prevent another outburst. Jack was her husband. Floyd was their friend. She needed them, perhaps more than ever.

She looked at the clock on the nightstand. 8:01. Randy was usually at the Institute during this time. Maybe she just needed to get out of this house and away from any reminder of that awful night. Randy was good about putting things into perspective.

"I'm going to the Institute." She pulled a long-sleeved shirt off a hanger from within the closet and slipped it on. Jack watched her, his eyes searching hers for an answer, a connection. But she was too heated to look at him. That worried her. To be angry with Jack was not something she'd ever really felt before. Frustrated, annoyed, sure. But angry? Jack had never given her reason to be angry.

As she looked at him, heat rose across her face and she opened her mouth to stay something, but she stopped herself. It would be too hurtful and she would hate herself.

On the way to the car, Rian wondered about her sudden flood of emotion. Why was she so upset with Jack? Her anger had been directed at Floyd, and rightly so. Yes, she had gone overboard when she'd yelled at him. Yes, there hadn't been any reason to shout at the messenger. But Floyd had seemed so supportive of the mayor's initiative. It pissed her off. And when Jack called her on her outburst, that had just flamed the tongue of fire.

Behind the wheel, as she peered through the thin sheet of fog floating in from the ocean, she was sure about one thing. She was justified for getting upset. It wasn't her style to yell at anyone, not even when she got worked up. Everyone who knew her described her as down-to-earth and reasonable. So that's how she knew that her feelings were somehow warranted. They had automatically, if not naturally, overwhelmed her, and Rian trusted that.

The front windows of the Institute were dark, but a soft glow emanated from one of the far rooms. She turned off the ignition and made her way to the back door. She had keys to all of the doors so she let herself in.

Inside, she heard humming from down the hall. Standing there for a moment, she tried to make out the lyrics. "There is no pain, you are receding. A distant ship smoke on the horizon. . ." Randy's voice was sharp and melodic. She frowned, not quite sure what the song was, though it sounded familiar. She stepped forward and stopped again as he continued singing. "Now I've got that feeling once again. I can't explain, you would not understand. . ."

When she turned the corner, she saw Randy bent over a table looking at something.

"Randy?"

His head jerked up as he jumped out of his seat, knocking the metal-backed chair hard to the ground. But as he recognized her, he let out a deep breath and placed a hand over his heart. "Rian, I didn't know you were here."

She laughed. "I just let myself in. I didn't mean to scare you."

He was laughing too. "I was just so focused on the. . ."He looked back at the table. "On, uh. . ." He was fidgety and hesitant. He covered his face in his hands and groaned. "Oh, I'm so embarrassed."

"What is it?"

When he removed his hands, he was smiling nervously. He motioned her to the table. A framed 4 x 6 photograph lay flat in the middle, surrounded by paperwork. The picture showed a close up side view of a young woman smiling, the rays of the sun fanning out behind her head. She looked like an angel.

"It's Jenna. Sometimes I really miss her."

She knew how serious he'd been about her. She touched his shoulder. "I'm sorry, Randy."

He shrugged and laughed and tucked the picture into one of the drawers.

"What was that song you were just singing?"

He looked confused at first, as if he hadn't realized he'd been singing out loud. "That was 'Comfortably Numb'. Pink Floyd. Something that makes me feel connected to Jenna. Well, that song is pretty bleak, I guess, but we used to listen to their songs together."

"I'm sorry."

He grinned. "Pink Floyd helps me get through it."

"Where's Shonda? Doesn't she usually work with you?"

"Yeah, but I sent her home. There wasn't much work to do." His tone changed as he turned to look at her. "I heard about the news."

"What news?"

"The mayor wanting to hire someone else to look into the shark attacks."

"How did you know?"

"Floyd told me. I think it's bull. You are the most clear-headed person I have ever met, and if anyone should be putting the pieces together, it should be you."

"Thanks, Randy. It means a lot to me."

He rose to his feet. "No, I mean it. I don't think Jack gives you enough credit."

"Jack?"

"I mean, lately, all I ever see him do is hover over you like you're a child or something, like you can't be left alone. The other day I tried to come over and he said it wouldn't be good for you."

"He did?"

"Yeah. I have to apologize for not being there for you. I tried, Rian, I really tried, but Jack kept pushing back. So I asked him to take care of you."

Rian recalled that night clearly. Jack said Randy told him to make sure she got some rest. She laughed.

"What's so funny?"

"I remember. He said you were being pushy, telling him to take care of me."

"I didn't mean to come across that way. I just wanted to get through somehow."

She hugged him. "You're a good friend."

He cleared his throat and shook his head as though embarrassed. "I gotta get back to work. I don't need Westen ringing my butt. I'll see you later." He switched the radio on at his workstation and turned the volume up as if to drown out his surroundings.

She frowned as she watched him turn his back to her. He'd cut off the conversation as quickly as a blinking eye.

***

They needed to make a move soon. Rian was remembering things that she wasn't supposed to remember. They thought they had ensured she'd forget, but the more she looked into the past, the more she put them in danger. If they didn't do something soon, it might be too late. She was getting too close to the truth.

***

When Rian crawled into bed, Jack didn't say a word. He gave her a soft kiss on the lips and turned off the lamp as he lied down to go to sleep. That was one thing she had always loved about him. He respected her need for distance. Better than that, he trusted her. That trust had been part of the foundation of their marriage. And it had never been broken.

Their bedroom housed a huge bay window. Through it a silvery shadow cast by the moon caressed the side of Jack's face as he slept. She touched his chest and watched her hand move in and out on top of it as he lied so peacefully on his side. Silently she criticized herself for the way that she had treated him. He didn't deserve her disrespect.

She placed her hand gently on his chest, it moving in rhythm to his breathing. Jack remained oblivious to the turmoil spinning inside of her that was building toward a climax that even she didn't quite understand just yet. Her heart swelled with love as she watched him lying there so at peace. But then it didn't. For a feeling of dread emptied it. She quickly took her hand back.

"Hovers over you like you're a child. . .can't be left alone." Randy's words pressed into her head like a warning. He had never spoken ill of Jack. He had never acted so distressed before. Why now?

Jack had been acting a little smothering lately and treating her like she needed someone to take care of her. It reminded her of this story written over a hundred years ago, "The Yellow Wallpaper", where this wife was misunderstood by her husband, a doctor, and how his treatment of her consisted of keeping her locked in a room "for her own good".

She pushed away from Jack. What if he thought she wasn't mentally stable now because of that November night or because of the shark attack? Maybe he called down all of their friends because he didn't know what to do with her anymore. She had lost it with him and Floyd, so it was at least somewhat reasonable that he might have these reasons for what he did. But the more she contemplated it, the more complicated her thoughts became, and the more confusing things seemed. She wasn't sure what to believe.

Somehow, she managed to fall asleep.

The next morning, she got started at the Institute early. She was actually able to concentrate and for that she was glad. She needed to forget everything for a while and just pour her mind into something completely unrelated to it all. To her surprise, Shonda came in to join her a little while later.

"I thought you wouldn't be in because of your night shift yesterday," Rian said.

The day was hot and Shonda wore white khaki pants and a navy blue top. Her black hair was tied back with a dark blue flower barrette. Even though she was in her thirties, she still looked like a teenager.

"I hadn't seen you in a while, so I thought I'd come in and chat."

"Yeah, I'm sorry. I guess I've been a bit stressed out about the shark attack. I haven't been really good company, honestly." She moved the notepad closer to the edge of the table. She worked on a blueprint most of the morning, something her boss, Westen, had thrown at her. It wasn't a normal part of her job, but he trusted Rian's opinion about some of the changes they were making and believed her perception was pertinent for some reason. She tried talking him out of it since her husband was more of an expert, but he responded that Jack's strength was in the physical construction, not the visual, as was hers apparently.

"What's that for?" Shonda peered over her shoulder.

"Westen seems to think that I'm an expert in engineering, so he wants my input about the layout of a tentative facility they're planning on starting next year."

"Must be nice."

"What is?"

"To be so revered."

Rian bumped her playfully with her elbow and they both laughed. Oh, it felt so good to laugh again. It made her realize how long she had been holding onto the pain of her situation. Situations.

"How's Jack's project coming along?"

"Good, I think. He hasn't really talked about it with me, too concerned with my well-being."

But was that really the reason? she now wondered.

"How are you, Rian?"

It was an easy question, but the answer seemed so complicated. "I don't know."

Shonda looked at her friend with concern. It was the same look everyone was giving these days. "Floyd told me about the mayor."

Rian curled her fingers tightly around the pen she was holding. Her heart thrust forward once. Twice. Like a boxing glove looking for a fight. "Apparently I don't have the mental capacity to match the damage of my own boat with the wounds of that boy."

Shonda placed her hand on Rian's. "No. Don't say that."

"Why not? That's essentially what Floyd said. What Jack believes."

"That doesn't sound like them."

"Shonda, ever since this. . .this shark attack, both of them have handling me like a broken vase. Even Randy notices. Jack wouldn't even let him come over the other day, like I'm some sort of invalid." She looked back at the paperwork on the table.

Shonda seemed to be thinking. "You know, maybe what the mayor is trying to do, well, maybe it will work. All this ambiguity might finally end and we will get some answers, some closure."

Rian appreciated her friend's optimism. "Maybe you're right."

"Well, if you need me, I'll be down the hall." She tossed her a smile. Rian turned back to her work and thought about going home. But she was still too angry. She realized that another reason she had chosen to come into work was to begin the process of calming down. Her anger had hit a high point. It wasn't a part of her normal nature to get so easily spun. By the time she left for the day, she wanted to be clear-headed enough to know which emotions she should listen to and which ones proved unfounded. She hoped for certainty by the time she got home.

Chapter Seven

~November 30 2013~One day after "the incident". Two years ago.

Rian was baking sugar cookies as Jack paced wildly back and forth from the kitchen to the living room to the bedroom and back to the kitchen. He was furious. He was scared. He wanted revenge.

Rian was energized and smiling as she pulled the first batch of cookies from the oven.

Randy lingered in the doorframe of the kitchen. His eyes followed her every move. He was worried about her. Why was she happy, he kept asking her, when she had just been nearly killed? He thought she was avoiding the situation and he worried what that might do to her.

Floyd spent most of his time philosophizing about the incident. The masked men had acted professionally. He thought it strange that they left just before Jack came home. His theory was that one of them might have recognized her. "We can't dismiss the possibility that they were tracking you guys, waiting for the right moment. It sounds staged." Floyd insisted that they must consider the possibility that one or both of them might know her.

Rian was too busy humming a Beatles song as she licked sugar off her fingers.

"Rian, come here." Jack finally came to a stop from his incensed pacing and gestured for her at the dining table. "Just take a seat. Breathe. Slow down. You need to process this."

"I'm fine." When she smiled, she could feel her ears sticking out and her heart leaping into the air. She really did feel fine, but even she knew it was weird to say so. "I don't know why, but I am!" She laughed at that. Some masked men had just hurt her, her head was wrapped in a bandage, there were blood stains on her shirt, and she was singing a song and making cookies.

She started to think she was turning into a crazy person, like some deranged villain out of one of Stephen King's stories. Maybe Annie Wilkes out of *Misery*, who saw herself as a perfectly reasonable and kind-hearted soul but who, in secret, liked killing babies and was torturing an innocent man. She shook her head at the thought. No. She wasn't crazy, of course. She was simply elated and she was glad about this feeling. If this was how she was going to feel, she could live with that.

"Jack, we should have her recall all the details of the event while they are still fresh in her head," Randy was saying. She heard their voices in the distance as if from inside a deep hollow of a cave. Then Jack was beside her.

"Rian, let's go through tonight and. . .". He looked around the room, stepped to the computer desk, and picked up a yellow tablet of legal ruled paper. "Write it down so we can make a report for the detectives."

She was more than willing to do so. So she began with her drive home. Just after her shift at the Institute, she met up with Floyd, Randy, Dylan and Shonda at a bar. About an hour later, she headed home. She carefully went through each moment as she came to it. The door opening, the masked mans' faces, the details of their clothes, all black, no part of their bodies visible. As she spoke, her body was relaxed and her voice was calm and confident.

"There were just two of them, but it seemed like more. They wouldn't leave me alone. They were all around me, their hands pushing me or grabbing me. The first guy, the one with the skeleton mask, demanded to know what I was doing there. He put a knife to my forehead and cut me, then he took the back of my head and shoved it into the wall. The black opal necklace that Jack gave me knocked against my chest as I fell to the floor." She looked over at Jack and saw sadness in his eyes. "It was his present to me on our first anniversary. He had it specially made with two one-karat diamonds on either side of it, to represent each of us, the opal representing our love." She grasped at her throat, but clutched at nothing. "When I was down on the floor, one of them asked for my jewelry and yanked the necklace off. I couldn't see much because the hall light was off. The next thing I knew the second guy was leaning down and telling me to put my hands flat on the ground. He kicked at my leg and told me to get on my stomach and stretch my hands out in front of me and to spread my fingers out. He reached under my stomach and grabbed my phone and keys. He stepped on my hand and asked if the ring was real gold, my wedding ring, and I told him it was and he told me to take it off. I tried, I tried so hard, but it wouldn't come off. The other guy walked away and came back with a wet washcloth full of soap. He told me to rub my hand with it until the ring came off."

Randy left to the kitchen and came back with a full glass of water. She drank a few sips and continued. Randy, Floyd, and Jack all sat at the table with her now, Jack holding her hand.

"They talked to each other for a while as I lay there on the floor. I couldn't hear what they were saying. They moved to the end of the hall and spoke in whispers. I kept thinking, 'Why isn't Jack here? Why did he have to work late tonight?'". She faced him and he smiled at her, squeezed her hand. "And then I started thinking how we shouldn't leave our front door unlocked ever again. It was such a funny thought in the midst of what was happening. It was a little too late for that!"

Recounting the event proved to be an easy task and she wanted them to feel as nonchalant about as she did. Instead, everyone was watching her with sympathy, waiting for her to go on. She cleared her throat. "Then I started feeling really tired. Anyway, the skeleton guy started walking back down the hall. He grabbed me by the hair and jerked me to my feet. Something wet got into my eyes. Blood was dripping from my forehead and falling onto my shirt."

The room turned really quiet. Regardless of the physical pain they had caused her, they couldn't take away her memory.

Floyd spoke up, a trace of worry in his voice. "You sound like a journalist simply reporting on some local entertainment news. Rian, I'm concerned about you. You have to let your feelings in."

Jack's voice came out quietly. "When I got home, you were asleep in our bed. I didn't want to wake you." He hung his head, a note of regret in his voice. "I had no idea something had happened to you."

Randy stared at her with sympathetic brown eyes. She smiled back.

After Randy and Floyd left a few minutes later, she remembered something. The detectives had found a single cigarette, a Lucky brand, in the driveway. Neither Jack nor Rian smoked. In fact, they didn't know anyone who did, so more than likely it belonged to one of the thugs. That cigarette might turn out to be the clue that would catch them. Rian found a bit of comfort as she typed up the report and emailed it to the detective.

After that, life for Rian rolled headlong into a series of fast-moving eccentric snapshots.

~December 1 2013~

Jack took Rian to Bayside Restaurant, their favorite place to dine, where they met Randy the year before and when, aside from Lilah and Luke, they started to develop all of their current friendships. The restaurant symbolized a place of happiness for Rian. Until now. From the moment they stepped into the establishment, she began to feel something she had never felt before. Emptiness. Disconnected from Jack, from her surroundings. Like she wasn't a part of anything or anyone. Not really here in any kind of way. Dead. Like she shouldn't be here. Yes, that was it. She felt like a ghost. Then she remembered the guns they'd pointed at her. How her life didn't flash before her eyes the way everyone who had a near-death experience always said it did. She had been able to feel only that this moment would be her last, and after that, nothing more.

"Let's get out of here." She was suddenly very uneasy.

Jack dropped his napkin on his dinner plate, paid the check, and ushered them both out of the restaurant and back home. She had never seen Jack so agreeable. Typically, he was an easy-going guy who didn't mind one way or the other where they ate or what they watched on TV or how they spent their afternoon. But here he was doing so much more than that, showing her how much he believed in her and her fears, even if he himself could not feel them. He didn't question her resolve to immediately leave. He just complied, knowing she needed to.

When they returned home, Champ greeted them, as usual, and Rian tried to smile at him, but she found that she literally could not do it. She followed Jack into the bedroom. "It should have been me," Jack said as he undressed.

"You couldn't have known they would be there."

"I should never have left you alone. I'm prepared for things like this. I was trained in the military for things like this. But you weren't. It's a good thing Luke's not here or we might find somebody who knows somebody." He came over to Rian and held her close, lovingly, protectively. "It should have been me," he mumbled once more. When he let go, she could see tears shining in his eyes. Jack wasn't one to cry, but he was crying now, in silence. His voice trembled as he said, "I almost didn't get to say goodbye."

She hadn't considered that fact before, what it must have been like for him. The mental agony and emotional torture thinking of the possibility that your spouse could have died. They'd had the opportunity to kill her. She'd been convinced that they would.

"I thought that was it, Jack. I didn't think I'd ever see you again. And you know what I felt? Nothing. I just thought, 'Well, this is it. My life is over.'" She hugged him. Tightly. For a long time. He pressed his mouth to her head, kissing it softly as she wept for the first time since it had happened.

After they let go, she pulled on soft blue pajamas and crawled into bed. Jack went to the kitchen for a drink of water. Her eye wandered to the window. It beckoned to her. She was sure that someone was going to drive by and rain bullets through the glass. She imagined the feeling to be akin to an experience much like going into a shark cage and hoping the shark would ignore her. The imminent threat clung to her like a dark fog, a shroud from which she could not escape.

But, somehow, she fell asleep as she heard Jack come into the room.

She was in the back passenger seat of her car and the man with the skeleton mask was driving, his partner sitting in the seat in front of her. The skeleton man sped through the parking lot of The Institute. She tried to open the back door, attempting to jump out, but it was too dangerous. It took her a while to figure out an alternate plan. He just kept driving through the parking lot. The next thing she knew she found a pencil in her hand and was stabbing the passenger in the neck, but nothing happened. He just laughed. He turned to face the driver and she stabbed him again, this time in his eye over and over and proceeded to pull his eye socket out before doing the same thing to the driver.

Rian was gasping and drenched in sweat when she woke from the terrifying dream. She grabbed at the blanket to shield her, as though someone were about to come at her. Her heart was beating like a jarring drum roll. She tried to breathe, but the weight of terror pushed down on her lungs. She looked over at Jack. He was sleeping peacefully. Rian wondered if her sleep would ever be pleasant again.

Chapter Eight

~December 2 2013~

The next morning at breakfast, she and Jack agreed that counseling would benefit her. He managed to schedule her an appointment for the afternoon.

He went with her to the office, waiting in the lobby while she met with her counselor.

Carly Ryder greeted her with professionalism, as she was expected to, but with an added dose of grace and personal interest. She extended her hand to Rian as she motioned to the couch and chair. "Your choice." Tucking her skirt beneath the backs of her knees, she sat in a black leather chair across from Rian, a clipboard poised on her lap. After the formalities were settled, the filling out of forms and the counselor's brief account of her availability, they began with the memory.

Rian relayed the details of the event, from start to finish, reciting the beats of the Black Friday, 2013, as though she had been programmed to. She couldn't yet reconcile the emotions with the occurrence, so the replay came out quite mechanically.

Carly introduced her to a technique called EMDR (Eye Movement Desensitization and Reprocessing), a form of trauma treatment. The therapy was less than thirty years old, having been discovered by Francine Shapiro in 1987 when, during a stroll in the park, she recognized that her eye movements reduced the negative feelings she had toward her upsetting memories. After conducting case studies, she discovered that the combination of eye movement and a cognitive module drastically altered the negative emotions associated with previous traumatic experiences. In essence, the anxiety connected to the event drastically diminished.

"We can start the therapy next time, but for today, I want you to share with me what's on your mind, why you are here."

Rian started with the unsettling feelings, the perception that something wasn't quite right, as if the darkness of that night was continually flooding back to her.

"When do you experience these feelings? What are you doing when they take place?"

Rian thought for a moment. They happened in particular situations. At the restaurant. At home. In her dreams.

Behind the sense of something dark lingering seemed to be the presence of a systematic planner.

"Based on everything you have told me, I can see that you have a minor case of post-traumatic stress disorder. The nightmares are a part of that. Right now, your senses are strong as evidenced in your dream. We will be working on reconciling them to the thoughts you have at the restaurant, at home, so that you can process them. In the meantime, I want you to think of a safe place."

Rian thought for a moment. "In the car, with Jack, me leaning on his arm as he drives."

"OK, good. So, when you start to experience those feelings of unease, focus on this place in your mind."

~December 9 2013~

It was her first day back to work. A group of students were being led by one of the other faculty members into a boat. SCMI had partnered with the Mountain and Sea Educational Adventures (MSA) organization in San Pedro in an effort to extend the student's learning experience. Every month, during the school season, over 1,000 students had the amazing chance to venture out in the Wilderness Explorer, which stayed docked at the Institute, taking trips to MSA's Science camps from Catalina Island in order to get a concrete feel for the marine environment.

Rian especially loved seeing the younger faces light up with excitement. The Institute often had students in lower elementary schools participate in the adventure. Last month's group had been able to snorkel and swim alongside schools of fish. Today they would be working in a bird lab, kayaking, and spending some free time swimming in Emerald Bay.

She crossed the grounds of the Institute, where she had worked for the past year, a familiar place, and yet a place she didn't recognize. Coworkers passed, waving or smiling at her. Groups of visitors made their way across campus innocently enough, but to Rian they looked suspicious, intent on doing something wicked, creeping to their destinations.

A man in his twentics strolled near her, in conversation with another young man. She found herself eyeing them suspiciously, convinced that they had been there on the darkest night of her life. One of the men was tall, the other average. Their physical descriptions appeared to match those of the masked men.

Her heart rate sped up. Her hands clenched. She thought of her "safe place", in the car with Jack, but the feelings of endangerment would not subside.

The men passed by her, paying her no attention. Rian kept walking, doing her best to forget them. They were just strangers who reminded her of the men who had hurt her. They had to be. She quickly made her way inside.

Shonda was glad to see her at work again and she asked how she was doing. Rian muttered that she was OK. But she wasn't OK, not at all. She moved over to her workstation and started working on a lesson plan for a future class of college students, but she couldn't concentrate.

As she headed home later that evening, she watched, with great trepidation, other drivers beside her, and she persuaded herself that one of them would turn to her with a gun in his hand, point it at her, and kill her.

~January 18 2014~

Rian and Jack drove to an In-N-Out drive-thru and ordered two burgers.

"I am so thankful for you, Jack. I love you so much." There were a lot of tears and the crying became more of an uncontrollable needy sobbing. She couldn't stop saying those same words to him four or five more times. It was like she had turned into a sphere of emotion all at once.

Jack took her hand and kissed her cheek. "I love you."

When they got home, Rian experienced similar feelings, only this time she was overwhelmed with gratitude for being alive. She was standing at the kitchen island and she just smiled as she cried.

And when they made love that night, all she could feel was happiness at being alive and being with her husband.

~March 3 2014~

To break up the monotony of going to work, Jack suggested they head over to the mall. "We need a break anyway. This project is turning out to be a lot more time-consuming than the Institute thought and you could use a day away, just having fun doing mindless shopping." He winked at her and she shook her head.

"If you wanted to go shopping, you just had to say so," she told him. Jack, not Rian, was the shopping addict. In fact, Rian hated shopping as much as she hated plucking her eyebrows. She did neither. But Jack loved shopping because it helped him relax. And he definitely needed to relax. Since that November night, he had been extremely protective of her, worrying about her every move. She had not gone anywhere without him at the wheel until last week. She could only imagine how the burden of that anxiety had overtaken him. He needed that break more than she did.

He kissed her straight on the lips and brushed his nose against hers, their own private expression of affection.

When they pulled into the parking structure, Rian was surprised by the number of cars parked in the lot. Today was a Monday, it wasn't a holiday, and it was ten thirty in the morning, when most honest people were hard at work.

Overhead, a few scattered clouds sailed through the sky, leaving behind a smudge of black specks. For the past several weeks, the weather had been nicely tempered, cooling the Newport Beach community with low sixty degree temperatures.

Once inside, they decided on an early lunch at a pizza place. Jack ordered a large pepperoni and pineapple, their favorite, and one large Pepsi for them to share. Rian found herself relaxing as they enjoyed their food and watched people walking in and out of shops. It was a mind-numbing experience, just what she needed to relax. After they were done, Jack went across the hall to a men's clothing store and Rian decided to browse for a pair of shoes a few stores down. She was actually having fun shopping for once. Maybe the mindless task of browsing was the right antidote. As she was about to pick up a pair of sandals, a loud screaming pierced the room.

Rian bolted upright and glanced around the store. A woman in her thirties was flying through the store, spinning her bags around in a frenzy. "Jamie! Jamie, where are you? What's happened to you? Oh my God! Jamie!" She was screaming so loudly that her words tumbled out in a wild slur of alarming panic.

When Rian looked around her, everybody continued their shopping as though nothing were happening, as if it were just a regular day at the old shoe shop when a crazy woman ran around in circles shouting at the top of her lungs. She couldn't believe how the customers just kept looking at shoes while Rian's heart jumped nervously. Or how the employees just looked on as if this were normal.

A moment later, the woman rushed into the fitting room and started screaming in a new kind of way, a sobbing release. Another woman in her thirties emerged from one of the rooms.

"Jamie!" The woman practically knocked her over as she threw herself into her. Jamie simply stood outside the fitting room door, adjusting her shirt and smiling at her. The back of Rian's neck tensed. The headache returned, pounding steadily. She was a mental wreck. The woman's behavior made her feel endangered. Why would someone come running through a store yelling like a crazy person? And why did nobody think it odd? She was all alone in a world where only she sensed the wrongness of things.

~April 7 2014~

"I saw a dream and it made me fearful; and these fantasies as I lay on my bed and the visions in my mind kept alarming me." Daniel 4:5

"Where do you want to go?" Jack asked as they dressed for the day.

"The Wedge." The Wedge was a romantic beachfront at the end of Balboa Island, a special spot for them ever since they moved here. But the second the beach came into view, the torrent of memories returned.

The skeleton man spoke first. "Move and I will blow your head off." He was pointing a gun in her face. He had her pushed up against the wall in the back family room.

The second man, wearing a shapeless black cloth over his head, grabbed her and dragged her to the bedroom where he shoved her face first on the bed. "Now it's time to go to sleep."

The skeleton man cocked the hammer. This was it. There was nothing after this moment. She would simply no longer exist. She wondered how Jack would be without her, how her friends would feel. What would life be like for them?

The masked men jerked away from her and quietly ran from the room, down the short hallway and out the back door.

Jack said he'd arrived just before midnight, minutes after she'd gone to sleep, minutes after they had gone. How close Jack had been to being a part of the crime. It was amazing how he had just missed them. She wondered what would have happened had he arrived just a little sooner. How badly would he have been hurt? Or maybe Jack would have hurt them both, gotten the cops, and none of this would be happening to her now. Not these feelings of being in peril or this certainty that death was coming to get her. Maybe if he'd been there just a few minutes before, they would be securely behind bars. But what good did it do to think such things? None of it was true.

Strangely, she felt elated, joyous a minute later. "I'm so thankful to be here with you." Rian started crying as Jack pulled into the parking lot of Balboa Island. He squeezed her hand. Her heart surged with fire as she thought about how precious life was and the wonder of still being in this world.

On the beach, Jack set up their chairs and a small table for their lunch. And then he took out a ring box. "I have something for you." She opened the box, and sitting on the black velvet cushion was a silver chain holding a black opal pendant framed by two diamonds, almost identical to the one that had been taken. "To replace the stolen one."

~April 14 2014~

Leaving work for the day, she walked by two teenaged girls, one of them wearing a sweatshirt that read "Gun Living". She looked again as the girls came closer and saw that it read

"Gun Living." That couldn't be right. They came within a few feet of her and she saw that it read "Cali Living". They passed her, engaged in busy chatter and oblivious to the edgy trepidation that came over her. Stunned, she kept walking to her car. How could she have misread that?

When she got home, Jack had the windows open so that a nice draft flooded through the house. After kissing him on the lips, she made her way down the hall when a sudden banging sound exploded behind her. She whirled and screamed.

"Sorry!" Jack opened the door to the kitchen. "The wind slammed it shut before I could grab it." He hurried over to her and held her close. She hugged him back, tightly. After several minutes, they pulled apart. Trying to normalize things, he whispered, "Sean and Kristen should be here soon for dinner. Randy and Floyd will be coming sometime later tonight too, just to hang out. They'll call when they're on their way."

A few minutes later, Sean and Kristen arrived. They came through the front door and entered the living room. Rian was in the kitchen and peeked out to say hello. Not three seconds later, she heard, "Hey!" and Sean was suddenly beside her. She screamed. Jack quickly came into the room to hold her.

"I'm sorry. I'm so sorry." Sean said to her. "I didn't mean to scare you. I thought you knew I was there." He touched her arm and his fingers were cold and sticky against her skin. Like the texture of blood. She jerked her arm away and looked at him suspiciously. He moved away from her, not knowing what to do.

"I know," she finally responded, though her heart pattered like a protective lion. She doubted his sincerity. He'd always been the quiet type. She learned over the years that the quiet ones were often up to no good. That's why being quiet was such a good cover. People didn't suspect you.

Dinner time was like listening to a silent movie. Everyone moved in hushed motions, keeping their eyes on the food, looking away from each other. It was awkward. Rian felt bad for her reaction, but only a little bit. Sean seemed embarrassed for surprising her, but that could just be an act.

After dinner, they returned to the living room to catch up with one another. As Rian listened to Kristen talking about the latest news with her company, her eyes kept wandering to the front door. Suddenly, she saw shadowy figures through the sheer curtains as they crept slowly up to the front door. She immediately stood up from her plate, walked straight to the door, and boldly swung it open. Floyd and Randy were standing on the porch.

Rian said, "Why didn't you call? You said you would call when you were on your way." She knew she was being reactive, a bit over-the-top, but thankfully they acted unperturbed.

"I'm sorry. We should have. We just thought you knew we'd be here in a little while so we figured it would be OK if we just showed up," Randy said. But his apology did nothing to settle her.

"You can't do that. You looked so scary outside, like you were slinking toward the house."

"We were just talking on our way in." Floyd smiled and hugged her.

She was amazed how composed they both were and how her uncharacteristic behavior didn't faze them. Like the mall, where she was the only one feeling disturbed while everyone else was calm. But she knew they were coming. She even recognized their shapes as they came up the walk.

Rian wasn't one to be so confrontational, she'd practically bitten their heads off, and yet they spent the evening with her as though she hadn't lost it a little. Indeed, they treated her no differently than before. She was thankful for that because she didn't know how to explain her rash reaction.

~June 13 2014~

Rian hopped on the computer and read a headline that disturbed her and made her heart sink to the floor: "Sixty-four-year-old man mugged by two young men". A video clip was attached showing an elderly man starting to pump gas into his vehicle when two thugs snuck up on him, knocked him to the ground, kicked him in the head, then took his wallet before running off. She instantly turned angry, indignant. A swelling pressure began forming in her skull and down the base of her neck. She touched her throat and her fingers lingered against the necklace that Jack had just replaced.

When she went to sleep, she had a very vivid dream where a strange woman reached out her thick white polished nails with black rounded tips. She raised one of her painted nails like a dagger and stabbed Rian in the forearm. "To numb you for twenty-four hours." Rian tried to get away as she cried out, "Why?!", but the woman refused to answer her.

She woke up in a cool sweat. Next to her, Jack continued sleeping, oblivious to the frightening dream.

Why were the nightmares returning? When would she be set free?

~July 7 2014~

For two hours straight Rian wanted to die. It was a feeling that Jack could not relate to, and though she told him about it, even he could only sympathize at best. Those two hours were the darkest hours for it was as if she were emotionally drowning, absent of all hope, and destined to a pathway of despair.

Later, her very real sense of terror was tested as she was sitting at the table reading a King novel and the lights in the kitchen suddenly clacked on. She jerked around in her seat and saw Jack. "You can't do that!"

"Hey, hey, it's   OK. I just turned on the lights. I didn't know that would startle you."

Rian dropped the book on the table and her head sunk into her arms as she sobbed. Jack rubbed her shoulders and kissed the back of her neck, but the warmth of his lips was overtaken by the cold damp sweat that tormented her entire being.

~September 19 2014~

It had been nearly a year since the Sheriff's Department had filed a report so Rian was surprised when an officer called asking her to come down to ID the suspects. Jack left work to come home and drive the two of them to the sheriff's station.

Officer Loyd was more than friendly as he led them to a back room. A long narrow wooden table sat at the center of the room and was sandwiched by two pairs of metal-backed chairs. Jack, at the officer's suggestion, waited outside in the lobby so as not to intrude or interfere with Rian's credibility or perhaps accidentally influence her opinion.

Rian sat down in the chair on the left, nearest to the door, because it made her feel better to be as close to Jack as possible. Officer Loyd placed the first sheet of pictures before her, all head shots. She had not seen the face of the shorter man because, of course, his face had been shrouded by a skeleton mask; however, she had been able to see a small sliver of the other man's neck, dark taut skin with fine wrinkles. She'd even mentally gauged his height as he lingered in the doorway. She had purposefully memorized the proportions of his height and weight, guessing him to be around two hundred pounds and about six foot two. She thought retaining such information was important.

She stared down hard at each profile, concentrating on each one for several seconds. There were four sheets of different profile pictures, thirty-two in total. She took her time letting her gaze travel from one image to the next, carefully examining the contours of the faces, the easy lines of their necks, the sharp edges, the shade of their skin. Most of the photographs contained men of Hispanic or Mexican descent. Out of the thirty-two images, only two pictures featured black men and three featured white men. But she was unable to recognize any of them. It was akin to looking for a black spider in a field of black spiders. They might as well all be one and the same.

The taller man had been wearing loose-fitting clothes and a large black cloth over his face, easy to conceal his true proportions. Remembering their height and the shape of the taller man's neck now seemed to be such pathetically and uselessly remembered details. She shook her head, frustrated.

"Don't be hard on yourself," Officer Loyd told her. "We may have them in custody regardless. There was another break-in a month ago and the DNA matches a glove that was left behind at your house."

Rian looked up feeling hope for the first time since all this had begun. "You found a glove?"

"Yes, but because it was found in the street, we can't be sure it belongs to the same guy. By itself, the glove isn't enough to secure the culprits. Do try to find comfort in the fact that we have the cigarette that was left in the driveway, and if we are able to lift fingerprints from it, that may identify your assailants."

When they left the station, Rian relayed her meeting to Jack, and as she did, her heart fell with despair a little bit more.

September 21st 2014

Rian dream about one of the thugs. He was in her house again, but this time he was lying on her bed. She called 9-1-1, but no one answered. She redialed, and this time someone picked up. She whispered, "Someone is here and is gonna try to kill me."

When she awoke, she didn't think much about the dream. There had been so many like them that she knew it was just a part of her processing the real events. She found a bit of comfort in the fact that, with each one, the situation progressed, that she was getting farther away from the danger. But there was another reason she didn't pay too much attention to the dream. She had been spending a lot of time in the Fish Lab at work and had a sudden desire to buy some fish.

"That's. . .different," came Jack's response to her request as he gazed up at her from his position on the couch.

She felt like a little girl as she squealed, "My first fish!"

"Really? I thought for sure you'd had one growing up. I mean, there was a rabbit, a cow, a lamb. . .but no room for a fish?"

"Ha. Ha. Do you want to come with me?"

"Nah. I'm going to sit here and root for the Broncos." On the TV, the Broncos were making a second quarter play against the Seahawks. Ordinarily, Rian would be lazing on the couch too, anything for a game of football, but she felt compelled to go to the pet store. Thankfully, it was open seven days a week and was just around the corner.

When she stepped into the pet store, that little girl in her came out again. She found herself turning in all directions as she gazed at everything the shop had to offer. Puppies. Kittens. Bunnies. Birds. Lizards. Mice. Hamsters. She looked at each and every one with delight.

When she came to three aisles of aquariums, her smile reached to the ends of her cheeks. There were loads of fish to see. So many varieties. She could hardly contain herself as she gazed into the first tank. At least fifty goldfish were swimming in circles, darting quickly back and forth, up, down, anxiously flitting from one end of the tank to the other. Though they were literally a dime a dozen, she couldn't help but feel that she gazed upon a treasure.

"May I help you?" A young woman wearing a company work shirt stepped up beside her.

"Anything in particular? We have every kind of fish here." Her smile was warm, inviting, as she gestured down the row.

"Oh, I don't know. It's so hard to choose. I just want them all."

She laughed. "My name is Trina. Please let me know if you have any questions."

"Thank you." She watched her walk away to attend to someone else.

The next tank held a type of fish that practically glowed. The label at the top of the glass read "Zebra Danio". Their blue striped bodies whipped back and forth as they hurried to the surface for their dinner. Rian watched some of the ones further below jerking their bodies, their beautiful blue shine gleaming.

The next two containers held scores of neon tetras, a softer golden color, actually more golden than the goldfish itself. Rian pressed her face closer to the glass, taking much pleasure in their constant swimming and diving. Then something dark popped up from behind the back of the tank.

At first Rian thought it might be one of those fake trees or some kind of plastic plant that often decorated the inside of the aquariums. But as her eyes moved from the tetra to the edge of the glass, she caught sight of two dark brown eyes watching her, eyes of a predator. Her heart burned from the intensity of the stare. Though she was free to leave the store, she felt trapped, like these fish, beneath the looming gaze of the unseen watcher.

"Rian?" A familiar voice spoke from behind the tank.

Rian closed her eyes, hoping she was wrong about her conviction, that he hadn't been stalking her, that he couldn't be one of the men from that night. And then he was behind her.

"What's wrong?"

She slowly opened her eyes and turned around to see Dylan. "Dylan," she whispered.

"You seem upset." He appeared genuinely concerned.

"I'm OK." Was she? He seemed like the same Dylan she'd known these past few years. Nothing weird about him. Perhaps the fish tank had distorted what she'd seen in his eyes. The water was a bit murky, so she could easily have mistaken his look for something more sinister.

"You looked at me like I had fins for arms and bulging eyes in place of a head."

She couldn't help it. She laughed. He always made her laugh. "Shonda with you?"

"No, she decided to visit her dad today. She sent me here because of my unprecedented genius ability to select the finest of goldfish."

"I'm picking out my first fish ever."

"Poor deprived childhood. A kid must have at least one fish in her lifetime. No, it's more serious than that." His dark features turned severe.

"What is it?"

"A young girl, fascinated by marine life, is, at the same time, terribly frightened by it. Her parents attempt to celebrate her seventh birthday by presenting her with a goldfish, but the young girl flees in terror, certain that this is not a harmless goldfish, but, in fact, a quarry bent on making her its next meal."

Rian laughed, loud and uncontrollably. What Dylan had said was a true story and he made it sound so much funnier than it had been for her at the time.

"I wish I had never told you. This image you have of me will forever be engrained in your head. I will be nobody but the girl who is afraid of her own vocation."

By the time they'd finished talking, the manager was ready to close the store and she forgot all about buying a fish.

"What did you get?" Jack asked as she walked through the door.

"Uh, nothing." She laughed at his confused face. "I ran into Dylan and we just kept talking and I forgot about getting a fish. He reminded me of my childhood experience where I freaked out about the goldfish my parents got me."

He laughed before changing moods. A rush of excitement reached the corners of his mouth. "I got a surprise for us, for our anniversary."

"That's two months away, Jack." She set her coat down on the bar and he moved close to her. "What is it?"

"That's no fun. Then you wouldn't be surprised."

Two months later, Jack surprised Rian with weekend reservations at a cabin up in Big Bear. The weekend passed by too quickly as it usually did when one was engaged in a particularly stress-free experience. Nonetheless, she and Jack renewed their pleasure in one another. Their love-making was ignited by a new sense of passion and they spent more time in bed than doing anything else.

Outside their cabin window, snow fell at a gentle and steady pace, frosting the edges of the pines trees and crystallizing the frame of the window. Jack had a small fire going in the fireplace, and they cuddled in each other's arms, finding more warmth in each other than from the flames of the hearth. And for a little while, just a little while, Rian felt safeguarded from the world.

Chapter Nine

Present Day: November 22 2015, three weeks after the shark attack.

Still relaxed from their tenth anniversary getaway, they practically collapsed at the foot of their bedroom, both of them drowsy and ready for a good long sleep, something they had done little of away at Niagara Falls, their first visit there, and hopefully not their last.

As it had done for the entire year, the window gazed at her like a portal into a dangerous world, waiting for someone to send pieces of glass flying into the air and a deluge of gunshots just for her. The window, for her, symbolized a villain, unmoving, permanent, rearing its ugly head. Strangely, she felt caught inside a horror movie, the stupid victim who always answered the door and ran right into the killer's arms. The smart ones ran for their lives, *away* from danger, not toward it. But she had to pass the window to get to into bed.

Slowly and with great trepidation, she allowed herself to move past the curtained window and into bed just as she had done many nights before. But this time the instant that she lied down to go to sleep, something horrible came upon her. A sudden and very overwhelming feeling attacked her being, both in the physical sense and in her soul.

Jack slid into bed beside her, but no comfort came of his near presence as it usually did. She was sure she was about to die, surer, even, then she had felt on that fateful November night.

She started sobbing. She didn't want to. She hadn't even expected to, but the tears came out of nowhere and they came so fast. Because it was like her very soul was dangling over the pit of hellfire, about to be set loose into the bowels of eternal nothingness.

She shared with Jack everything she was feeling. He held her softly and reminded her of his love, of God's love. But she didn't feel comforted at all, for within moments, those same certain convictions became horribly unbearable. She would no longer be here in the only world she had ever known. And it wouldn't be because of any gunshot. Bullets would not come shattering through the windowpane. Instead, she would just stop breathing.

More tears came and they refused to stop.

For two years, she had struggled with feelings of endangerment, but nothing like this. She wasn't putting these thoughts into her head, something had a hold of her. It had taken control of her mind and her spirit. She could feel nothing but this terrible feeling of finality. Her crying quickly built into a crescendo of helpless moaning.

"No!" she screamed through a flood of burning tears. "I want to stay!"

Jack had never been a man of prayer, but suddenly he was praying.

For two hours she suffered, oppressed by the certainty that her life was about to be taken. Then, in a single second, the suffocation ended. Gone. Just like that. No more tears, no more indication of pending doom. All of the sensations and thoughts disappeared, mysteriously, in an instant.

The next morning, she asked Jack, "What happened to me?"

"I don't know, baby. How are you now?"

"Like it never happened."

"I think you should see Carly again."   He was right, but she was so angry at having fallen backwards, far beyond any place she had been before since this terrible nightmare had begun. Greater than the anger was this sense of bafflement. What had she just experienced?

It was more than difficult to concentrate at work. Randy and Shonda noticed something was different about her right away. She told them both about last night. After that, both of them kept trying to persuade her to leave. After lunch, she finally did.

"Just go home and get some rest," Shonda suggested.

"Shonda's right. You should get some rest. You're trying to do too much," Randy said.

"Actually, I have an appointment today with my counselor. Jack thought I should go, considering what happened last night. It's probably related to that event."

He looked concerned. "Do you think that's the answer? You might just need a good long nap to put everything in perspective."

"No. That's never happened to me before. It wasn't anything normal. I really thought I was going to die right then." Her body shook a little at the memory.

Randy reached out to take her hand. "I'm sorry. I just don't want anyone forcing you into something." He quickly left as though the conversation had become too painful for him to continue. She stared after him, confused. Why was he acting so protective lately?

When Rian left work, it was mid-afternoon. Above her was a strange sight. It was like someone had dragged his nail across the sky, puncturing the blue firmament with a razor-sharp white line. Cutting into her, like that night. She shivered. Where had that thought come from? She had never had it before. Why now? Why was the memory haunting her again? Whatever the reason, she knew that every element of every moment of that night had become an indelible reminder of how tenuous the years of her life were.

Her whole life she had lived as though there were an endless supply of tomorrows, as if death did not exist. And now, in almost every day that followed the night that had altered her world, the end of her days seemed to teeter on the brink of a last breath, and she felt the certainty of the fleeting length of this life as she knew it. But much more than all of that, she felt that death, at least the very idea of it, was no longer some abstract concept or something that just happened to other people. Now, death had become something very real, lurking with tangible imminence, crouching behind the next corner in wait for her.

When she got to her car, the headache had returned. It pressed harder into her skull than ever before. She closed her eyes tightly and placed her hands on her head as if to prevent the pounding. After some minutes, the pain subsided. She got into the car.

As she drove along the highway, she thought about her marriage. Could it withstand the stress she had been under? She had pushed Jack away out of frustration. She didn't altogether trust him. He had said that he'd left early to go to the store for some wine and steak sauce that night on the way home from work. He'd carried those items in a brown paper sack when he came through the door. But it was so convenient. The timing so timed. Only minutes between the moment the two men left the house and Jack walked through the front door. How could that be a coincidence?

When she pulled up to their house, she felt ashamed for thinking these things. Jack had never given her any reason to doubt him. What possible motive could he have to hurt her anyway? He had always been a gentle, kind, and loving man to her.

When she got inside, Jack looked beyond relieved to see her. Without saying a word, he moved out from behind the kitchen counter where he was prepping dinner and embraced her. She allowed herself to fall into his arms, closing her eyes to savor the moment and to block out the doubts. When they at last pulled away, his sea-green eyes flashed tenderly. "I missed you."

"I know. I. . .". She wanted to return the same words. As if sensing her hesitation, he pressed his fingers against her lips, excusing her reluctance, having compassion on it, and went back to the kitchen to resume dinner. Champ padded over, softly whimpering as if he detected that something wasn't quite right.

Hours later, just as they finished their meal, someone knocked on the door. Jack left the kitchen and Rian could hear Floyd speaking and other voices coming down the hall. A moment later, Jack and Floyd came into view alongside Dylan and Shonda.

"Hey, kiddo!" Dylan gave her a hug and it felt as comfortable as it always had. "Are you sure you should be in the kitchen? I don't want to have to call the fire department." Rian slapped him playfully and he laughed.

Hey, sweetie," Shonda said. "Did you find room for a nap yet?"

"Actually, I've got to get going to my appointment." She glanced down at her watch. The four of them looked at her with concern, but she pretended not to notice as she waved goodbye.

"We'll be here when you get back," Floyd said.
***

He was disgusted with her. He had consoled himself with the plan for the time being, but he was growing more impatient with waiting. Her presence served only to sting him and remind him of how inadequate he was. She wasn't going to let him forget it. He *hated* her.
***

Carly did a session of EMDR with her. They began with a time when Rian felt like she was not in control. It was during her college years, when there seemed to be no light at the end of her academic world.

Carly explained. "It's best to go back to something less traumatic, something more manageable but with similar associations, like this feeling of not being in control. From there, we move forward to the event. This way, too, you are able to process these experiences together since they share a similar feeling."

Sometime in the middle of the session, she found herself back at the beginning, with the masked men and their cruel hands as they shoved her through the door and up against the wall. It was the first time that the memory became real. No longer some abstract thought spinning in a far-off abyss. Now she was connected to it with all of her body and mind.

She closed her eyes. Something else had happened that she couldn't quite grasp. Her eyes flicked open. "The dream."

"Tell me about the dream."

"I'm in the ocean. There's nothing around me at first. I think I'm all alone. But in the next moment, I see a baby tumbling in the distance. I swim closer, but the more I push forward, the farther the baby moves too. Frustrated, I stop. I reach out my hand toward the baby, but it vanishes."

Rian's breathing was hardly audible, but she could feel the air in her lungs pushing hard and fast. The chair was nicely upholstered and she dug her fingernails into the arms of it as she struggled against the shallow breaths. Her skin felt like it was on fire. But the worst pain was in her forehead, not unlike the headaches she had been experiencing.

"OK, take a deep breath, Rian, hold for five seconds, and let it out slowly."

She did as Carly told her. Then again, twice more.

Her breathing slowed down as her arms sagged into a resting position, her fingers unclenching from the arm rests. Her body temperature had cooled down too, back to normal.

"Tell me what you noticed."

"I feel tightness throughout my body, but mostly it's here." She pointed to her forehead.

"That's where you probably hold most of your tension."

"And my breathing was shallow the whole forty-five minutes we were doing this."

"When else did you experience a time where your breathing was like this?"

"Just over five years ago, actually. My dad died. He had a heart attack. They couldn't save him. My mom started flinging hospital trays, magazines, anything she could get her hands on, at the nurses and doctors. It was too much for me and I almost stopped breathing. Jack had to rush me to the ER."

"I want you to think of a place where you feel safe. Take a moment, if you need to. It can be in the car with Jack or somewhere else."

"The last time I tried thinking of us together in the car, I just got more anxious."

"Try somewhere where you are alone, at peace."

That was easy. "My workstation."

"When you start to feel anxious, I want you to visualize yourself at your workstation and concentrate on a word or a small phrase to alleviate that anxiety. For at least twelve minutes, meditate on this word as you picture your safe place. This will enable you to link your thoughts to your emotions instead of compartmentalizing them. Or, if you are somewhere where you are stationary, you can go through those relaxation body movements, starting from the top of your body to the ends of your toes, as you were instructed in your earlier sessions."

"What about my dreams?"

"The nightmares you have had and the anxiety are all related to your PTSD, but I believe we will be able to alleviate those symptoms after a few more sessions. Take care of yourself and remember to call me if you should need anything before our next meeting." She smiled at Rian and walked her to the door.

When Rian returned home, all of them were talking animatedly on the couch and looking at her in unison as she walked through the door.

"The mayor would like to meet with you in the morning," Jack said.

"We can all go with you." Shonda stood up.

"You know what? That would be great, actually."

Thanks to Jack, their friends caught wind of her visit with the mayor. Lilah and Luke couldn't come out, of course, but they called Rian to remind her that they were with her in spirit. The rest of their friends met up with her and Jack at the front door. Even Hal was there. And, as if brilliant beyond even human capacity, Champ sniffed at her and yelped as he pawed at her jeans to demonstrate his excitement.

"Thank you, Champ. We'll get this all figured out. Don't you worry." Rian ruffled his hair around and kissed his nose.

It was a chilly morning and the fog came rolling in thick clouds over the island. Jack held her hand while Dylan and Shonda kept pace behind them. Rian noticed a tension between Sean and Kristen and wondered what it was. Sean was typically quiet, but he was more than that this morning. He had been brooding, and Kristen, usually the one to lift everybody's spirits, looked downtrodden. They used to never be able to take their eyes off each other, but neither one of them had looked the other's way the entire morning. Rian supposed she shouldn't be too concerned. Some of them were having sympathy pains for her, like Floyd and Randy who kept asking her if she was OK. They were reminding her of overprotective parents, which normally would have irritated her, but in this moment made her feel a bit more at ease about this whole situation.

"Don't let him kick around the bush," Dylan broke the silence.

"Don't you mean beat around the bush?" Jack said.

"No, these guys tend to come kicking and screaming."

Everyone laughed at that. Even the tension between Sean and Kristen faded. Some of them started chatting and Jack released her hand and stepped back to join Floyd and Randy.

Though Jack and her friends were just steps behind her, she suddenly felt alone on the island. That horrible sensation that she was in danger returned to her with a mighty punch. Her chest tightened and her breathing slowed. A heavy pressure began to build across her back. The impact of the shark attack had bruised her chest and back, so the pain made sense. But something about it was different this time. She moaned as she rolled her shoulder forward in an attempt to lessen the pain.

Remember the workstation. Your safe place. It came to her. The smell of the ocean drifting through the window. The feel of the keyboard. "Peace. . . Peace. . . Peace," she chanted softly.

As they came to the end of the walkway, she continued to softly repeat the single soothing word. Her body began to relax.

Mayor Koontz was waiting with a small group of people, some photographers, others probably there to enjoy the press coverage, and a two-man news crew. Koontz was all business. In a dark blue suit and navy blue tie, he camouflaged with the ocean. He held out his hand by way of greeting. If ever he had been a chatty sort, it must have been long ago, his feelings for humanity lost somewhere in his days of youth.

"Rian, Jack, thank you for coming." He glanced behind them with firm disapproval. "This isn't a parade."

Floyd stood still, keeping his eyes on the mayor. Rian regretted having been angry with Floyd before. He had only been the messenger, and clearly, by the way he held his ground against the mayor, he was there to support her. Koontz turned away. "The Marine Biologist will be coming this afternoon. Jimmy Woods, the teenager who was attacked, will be here any moment, so let's have a look at the Sundancer."

The boat had been ferried over to an onshore plant in preparation for this very day. The group of them walked down the promenade for a few yards until they arrived at their destination.

The *Freedom* looked terrible. Unlike the pristine condition in which they had purchased it, it now resembled a boat of shambles. On the night of the attack, it had been too dark for Rian to see the details of the damage, but now, in the glint of the morning sun, it was all too clear. On its right side, dead in the center, was a large punctured hole, not a perfect hole but a jagged shredded chaotic nightmare as though something had chewed right through it. That something being the shark.

She shivered and closed her eyes, but she could not stop the icy sensation that curled her skin. It was here again, the feeling from before, that certainty that something lurid was lurking nearby.

A photographer stood next to Koontz, snapping pictures of the damage. Rian looked behind her. Everyone was staring at the boat, most of them in shock since this was the first time they had seen its condition. But something wasn't right as she looked at each one of them. The suspicion and the worry and the dread she had known before came roaring back now with a fierce certainty. Someone here wanted to hurt her. Her heart shuddered. Not a stranger, but someone she *knew*. Now she was convinced that it was someone familiar because she felt personally violated. The memory of that winter had been buried through therapy, through denial, and now it was coming back with an inevitability that the two men had not been random outsiders, but people who were already in her life.

Before he died, her dad had always stressed the importance of trusting your instincts. He'd said that doing so had saved him from the deception of others. Rian had loved her dad immensely and embraced this bit of advice from him that she had cherished even after he'd died.

As the clicking of the camera continued, she looked over each person in the group as though observing them for the first time. Jack was beside her, talking to Hal. His eyes were glued on Koontz as they spoke. Stress was creasing the span of his forehead and the green in his eyes were afire with frustration. He didn't look like the same Jack, the one who was usually in control and at ease. After ten years of marriage, had something changed within him? She couldn't forget the couple of remarks Randy had made that had put Jack into a different light, a bad light. But the more likely reason, the one Rian hoped to be true, was that his furrowed brow and steely eyes were in response to the stress of this situation.

Hal was next. The grandfather she had never had. Since their move here three years ago, he had been nothing but sweet, as sweet as his candy shop. She had no reason to doubt him. Still, she didn't want to rule anyone out if she was going to come to the truth. She may not yet know why one of her friends might want to hurt her, but her suspicion was real, and she had no reservations about it. His eyes twinkled as he glanced at her and continued talking to Jack. Was his friendliness genuine or a hoax? She didn't know. And she had to consider that she had only known him for a relatively short period of time, just as long as the rest of them, except for Jack.

Kristen was behind them, looking around the dock as if she were searching for someone. She and Sean hadn't been on good terms. Sean had his eyes on the ocean as if deep in thought. Rian wanted to ask them what their fight was about, but she didn't want to sound overeager. It wasn't her style to intrude. But Sean was reticent, and behind that tendency to be less communicative might be a hidden intention never suspected.

It sounded ridiculous, even to her own ears, to think that her trusted friends were seeking to harm her. She knew that the idea of any of them wishing to put her in danger was a wild idea that had seemingly come out of nowhere. But it hadn't. It had been there ever since the night of the shark. That's how she thought of it now. "The Night of the Shark". She was getting closer to discovering who was after her. But what kind of harm did they intend to inflict? That, she had no answer for.

She looked further down the boardwalk, at Dylan, who was always cracking jokes and making light of things. Even right now, as Koontz and the photographer finished wrapping up the session, he was making Shonda and Randy laugh. But maybe his wit was just a way of hiding something. Maybe he wore that mask to make sure that he could get away with something as evil as murder, knowing no one would ever suspect his dark motives.

Randy, just like the others, had been a good friend too. But lately he had been a bit overprotective of her. Why was he suddenly so worried about her? And why didn't he trust Jack? Maybe he recognized something distrustful in Jack and was trying to protect her, or maybe he was trying to make Jack look guilty to make himself look trustworthy.

Rian pressed her hand to her head, which had begun to throb. The thought of any of them wanting to threaten her was too painful to deal with, but she knew she had to.

Floyd was the last one. Always a thinker, he had a flair for language, a way of making things sound better than they might be. Were his euphemisms for any given situation his stealthy way of misleading her down a path of peril? Maybe his kinship was just a way to get Rian to trust him so that she could easily be deceived.

She swallowed the dryness in her throat and stared back at Koontz, who was motioning to her. He pointed at the side of the Sundancer. "Here we can see the size of the teeth. Mr. Dreyfuss will be here soon, like I said, and he'll be able to give us a clearer picture of things. Once we have something solid, I'll be in touch with you, no later than this evening." He turned slightly and called out to a young boy. "Over here, Jimmy."

Jimmy Woods was a fourteen-year old black kid of small stature with thin arms and knobby knees. His smile was almost as small as he was, but in it was a serenity that Rian missed from her own life. She introduced herself and they smiled at each other, and Rian's heart soared a bit at the thought that their similar experiences might lead to solving this mystery.

Mr. Woods was a large man with bulging muscles and a smooth approachable face. She shook his hand.

"How are your injuries?" She turned back to Jimmy.

He lifted his shirt to reveal deep wounds. Three almost perfectly sharp lines shined against his dark skin. Rian shook inside and tried to remain calm for Jimmy's sake. Though the leg work had not yet been done, Rian knew that the shark that had damaged her boat was the same shark that had hurt Jimmy.

"He's getting better, though. On the road to recovery!" His dad piped in as he squeezed his son's shoulder. Rian nodded.

As if in a spell, she felt drawn to *Freedom*. She inched forward, past Jimmy and his dad, past the photographer, then Koontz who was standing at the edge of the dock. She wanted to get a closer look, just to be sure.

"Was it just the side of the boat?" Koontz asked.

"No, there's some damage on the stern as well." Rian stepped closer to the boat.

"Hey, Mr. Dreyfuss, let's get a couple more shots in before you head out," Koontz called out to a gray-bearded man. "We got some more damage on the stern. Let's get an angle from inside, then we'll get the boat turned around and get a few more shots from the outside."

Mr. Dreyfuss nodded, stepped into the boat, and began clicking away again.

***

The shark moved its colossal sleek body rapidly through the ocean. Its fin sliced through the top of the water as it pressed straight toward the boat. The distance shortened until only eight more yards separated it from the moving object ahead. Half a minute passed before it closed in. Four yards. One yard. SMACK! It burrowed its face into the side of the boat. It had reached its destination.

***

Just as the photographer snapped the last picture, a huge blast of water sprayed up through the air. Everything happened in slow motion in that instant. Dreyfuss lost his balance, falling backwards onto the floor of the boat, his camera spinning like a tetherball around his neck. Koontz held his arms out toward him as though trying to stop the geyser. Jack turned from Hal, his mouth dropping open, his arms reaching for Rian to pull her away from the water's edge.

The tunnel of water appeared to freeze as though it had erupted into a large gaping mouth of sharp-horned teeth. She immediately recognized the teeth. She would never forget them. This was her shark.

That night, alone in *Freedom*, she had been unable to scream right away. The shark made sure to thrust its powerful body against the vessel, keeping her flopping and throwing her all over the boat. She hadn't been able to catch her breath, much less process what was happening at the time. Everything happened too fast.

Just like that Black Friday.

That night on the boat, she hadn't found her voice until the shark had nearly torn her foot off. But now she screamed with a deeper sense of terror than she'd ever known. The vibration of the scream reach way down into the depths of her being.

Things stopped moving in slow motion like someone had pushed stop on a tape recorder. One second. Two. Then time sped up.

Dreyfus steadied himself against the steering wheel. The shark rammed its nose into the Sundancer. Dreyfuss toppled over the seat behind him as the shark dipped back into the water. Koontz and Hal rushed over, grabbed Dreyfuss, yanked him from the boat. All three landed feet first on the dock. The shark flashed its fin as it swam off. Jack hugged Rian close to his body. Kristen cried in Sean's arms. Dylan and Shonda came to Rian's side. Randy flinched as he stared at the shark. Hal sheltered Rian from the water side of the dock. Floyd gasped, in a state of shock. Then time returned to normal.

No one could have known, of course, that the shark would be there. So why did Rian feel so sure that someone was behind its reappearance? An absurd thought. But she knew, somehow she just knew that someone here had orchestrated the event, timed it to absolute perfection.

Koontz had been the one to set the time of the meeting. Could it be him?

She looked away from Jack to see Koontz and Dreyfuss still shaken up, Hal trying to calm them both down. Koontz was already on the phone with the police, his eyes warily glued to the ocean. It was unlikely he wanted to risk her life. And he didn't know Rian well, certainly not on a personal level. And for whatever reason, Rian knew that whoever was after her was close to her.

Someone here wanted to hurt her. Had already hurt her. Her hands became shaky as that new realization hit her. Two men had attacked her on Black Friday, changing the meaning of that unofficial holiday forever for her. It made sense why she felt endangered lately. Because the two thugs weren't strangers. Though the ideas she'd been forming in her own mind over the last several days weren't entirely clear, they would be, she knew they would be, once she had all the pieces in place. Her next thoughts sounded far-fetched, perhaps even paranoid. None of it yet made sense, but the chance that the shark would be there, at the exact location, precisely moments after she'd arrived, was not coincidence. It was intentional.

Rian laughed inside. What she was thinking was outrageous. Because what she believed required an illogical theory, one that, even with all the time and tools in the world, could not have been put together so efficiently. The theory called for drastic measures, so if someone wanted to scare her, they must be able to concoct a plan that entailed mechanical manipulation. A kind of technology that allowed control over a shark's movements. Aside from a number of B movies, Rian didn't think that possible.

She looked back to Randy, who was talking quietly to Floyd, apparently processing what had just happened. He caught her eye, winked, and turned his attention back to Floyd. Was that a menacing wink? Were he and Floyd discussing the next part of their plan?

"What is it?" Jack whispered into her hair. He took her hands in his, trying to calm her.

Intentional.

A chill crept across her neck. The opal necklace was cold against her skin. Two Novembers ago had been intentional in ways she hadn't realized before. Today's shark surprise had also been intentional. And, in some kind of mysterious way, the two incidents were related. She had to tell Jack, even if she suspected him. If he was innocent, they could work together, and she was willing to take that risk.

"Both nights are connected. Don't ask me to explain how. I can't. Not yet. But I know that they are tied together in some way," she whispered. She looked over at Jimmy Woods and his dad, both who were in a serious conversation with Koontz. Mr. Woods looked angry, but at whom she wasn't sure.

She turned back to Jack. "It took almost a year for the DNA results and they came back with nothing. These guys weren't amateurs. They knew what they were doing, which is why the police never found anything. Not a single fingerprint or hair." She heard the anger rising in her voice.

"What about the cigarette?"

"Maybe one day, when I'm dead."

"Rian!" Jack touched her face. He knew she needed to leave. "Let's go home." Their friends hugged Rian as they said their goodbyes. By the time they walked to the end of the walkway, the police had already arrived, their spinning red lights wailing.

Chapter Ten

Back at home, at Jack's urging, Rian called Carly for an emergency session; she had an opening that afternoon. In their living room, next to a warm fireplace, Jack attempted to soothe Rian. He poured them two glasses of red wine, made a plate of cheese and crackers, and turned on her favorite music at low volume, but his efforts were in vain. What Rian needed was sleep, a good long sleep that would take her from this wretched morning and plunge her into a world of escape. She was mentally and emotionally saturated with the morbidity of both events, no, make that all three events now, and with the creepy feeling that someone close to her wanted her dead.

Jack gently tucked her in and made sure the bedroom was heated to her satisfaction before he left to the kitchen. By the time she woke up, she was relieved that she had slept without having any nightmares.

After sharing the horrifying events of yesterday's shark event, Rian agreed with Carly that she was ready to resume the EMDR therapy. This is where she would concentrate on a vivid part of that experience as she thought something negative about herself, something that the experience and the men had prompted her to feel, even though it wasn't true, while finding a positive belief to replace it and noticing the emotions and sensations in her body.

"We're going to go back to the earlier event now because yesterday's is too fresh, too strong. We need to ease our way up to it." Carly handed her a chart with about forty different negative statements about one's self. Rian carefully read through each one and found one of them to be particularly relevant—'You have no control'.

Carly pointed two closed fingers in between them and slowly waved them back and forth, like a pendulum. As in prior sessions, this continued for about thirty seconds with Rian following her fingers using just her eyes as she focused on the skeleton mask, the primary thing that she had seen. At the first stop, she reported that she felt her hands grow a little tense. She wasn't able to identify any particular emotion. It still wasn't easy, the therapy, to connect the feelings to the thoughts. They felt like two very separate things that could not be joined together. She told Carly this.

"It can be difficult to link these two items. In your earlier sessions, you dealt with the trauma by separating your emotions from the event. It's a defense mechanism. Trying to associate the thoughts and feelings will be a bit challenging, but it will come. Just don't force anything."

She held her fingers up again and rotated them back and forth, slowly at first, now rapidly, as if symbolically dispelling any negative thoughts Rian had about herself.

The mask loomed again, so close, like a zoomed in face. Her hands became tense once more, tightening into small orbs of iron. But this time her heart also began to race. *You are not in control.*

Carly paused, told her to take a deep breath. "What did you notice?"

"My hands felt tight, almost numb. My heart started to beat really fast."

"On a scale from one to ten, with ten being the greatest, how would you rate the belief that 'You are not in control'"?

After a few seconds, Rian said, "Eight".

Carly noticed Rian's disappointment. "It's nothing that can be forced. Now, I want you to replace that with a positive statement about yourself. What might that be?"

"That I am in control."

Carly nodded and resumed the swaying fingers.

This time something new happened. She saw the mask and felt the gloved hands and they pushed her face first into the wall. Her arms twitched at the memory and the beating of her heart began to rise. She gasped. Remember your words. 'You are in control'. She silently repeated the phrase.

After several seconds, Carly stopped, instructed Rian to take a deep breath, then asked for her response.

"I moved past the mask this time." She knew from previous sessions that this sometimes happened quite naturally, especially when body sensations and beliefs about one's self were explored. "Hands started grabbing me and someone shoved my face into the wall. The tension was there in my arms and heart rate increased again."

"How would you rate the belief that you are not in control?"

Rian felt better this time, though not where she wished she were. It was hard to convince herself that she was in control when there was so much about that moment that remained a mystery. "Six".

Carly went through a few more oscillating gestures and by the time they neared the end of the session, Rian was at a "five".

"This is wonderful. You started at an eight and are already at a five. You're making good progress, Rian. Make sure that you continue to meditate on your word daily. Also, focus on your safe place when you need to. Note any dreams, negative body sensations or thoughts, etcetera, in your journal. Call me during the week if you need me before our next visit."

When Rian got home, Jack was sitting at the bar, his hands curled around a shot glass. He didn't drink often, so Rian knew that he was worried, stressed. He got up when he saw her, kissed her tenderly on the lips, and pulled her close to him. She buried her face into his chest, closing her eyes in an attempt to block out the sight of her surroundings. After all, this is where it had happened, right here in the hallway, just a few feet away.

He took her to the bedroom and they made love for the first time in many days. Afterward, she felt refreshed in both body and mind. The act of love had brought a cure, albeit temporary, by flushing the gossamer of black remembrances. She lied on the bed throughout the afternoon with Jack and they simply held each other. It was all she needed.

Later on, Lilah called from Maryland. She told her Luke had been promoted and they would likely be moving to California. But she had mostly called to check on the meeting with the mayor. Rian filled her in. "What? Are you OK? No one got hurt, did they? Oh my God, Rian. Oh my God!"

Rian wished Lilah were here. Maybe she would feel normal again. After she finished telling her the strange things she'd been feeling, Lilah took a deep breath.

"You have to go to the police."

"Lilah, with what? Proof of my emotions? They'll laugh me out of the station or handcuff me."

"No, sweetie. Because of the shark poses a threat to everyone. They need to shut the beach down until it is caught."

Rian's cell phone rang. It was the mayor. "Lilah, I'll call you back. It's the mayor."

"Mr. Koontz, what's the word?"

"I met with the Marine Biologist, and after going over the damage of your boat, little Jimmy's wounds, and the shark from today, he's concluded that this is, indeed, the same shark."

Rian thought about Lilah's comment. "I want the police contacted and the beach shut down."

"This isn't a Spielberg movie, Mrs. Field."

She ignored the snide remark and the irony that he was reacting in much of the same derogatory way that the mayor had toward the chief of police in *Jaws*. "How big is it?" The

Great White in *Jaws* was twenty-five feet long and weighed three tons.

"He estimated it around twenty feet and about 4,000 pounds. The bite radius matched Jimmy's to your boat's— three feet wide. He said that it's not uncommon to have them swimming these waters, but that to find one so close is. And it's been years, he says, since someone has been hurt." He said it matter-of-factly as if any of that downplayed the severity of what had just happened.

"I want the beach closed and the chief of police contacted. And if you don't do that, I will go to the police myself." The tension in her body was building just like it had during her last EMDR session, and the tapping of her heart was building rapidly into a crescendo of brass and winds. Relax. Relax. Relax. She had to start concentrating now. Where was her safe place? Oh, yes, her workstation. Relax. Relax. Relax. She slowly began to feel the hard beat of her heart subside and the tension in her hands forming into a tingling sensation.

Koontz broke into the cacophony. "I'll take care of it. You will hear from one of us soon."

Rian called Lilah back, quickly reported the update, and hung up. She was in no mood to talk. Jack was in the shower. She continued her mantra as she looked down at her watch. Ten more minutes. Relax. Relax. She closed her eyes and heard the spraying symphony of the running water and it further alleviated the strain in her body until it was gone.

"Was that the mayor?" Jack came out wrapped in a towel, the blond spikiness of his hair glistening.

"He's getting a hold of the police as we speak. I've asked him to close that area of the beach."

"Do you think the chief will comply?"

"Yes."

Champ trotted over to her and nudged at her hands as if sensing that's where she was hurting. She rubbed his head and finished silently chanting the last two minutes of her meditation. Being surrounded by Jack and the dog's affection soothed her so that she could almost believe that the shark attacks hadn't really happened and that her certainty that two people close to her were involved in that night, that maniacs were among her close inner circle, was a whimsical figment of her imagination.

When Mayor Koontz phoned her again, she wasn't prepared for what he told her. "The Chief is shutting down Balboa Island until this shark is found and killed. He wants to meet with you at the station immediately."

Jack drove the two of them down to the police station, a few miles away. Rian was confident that this whole nightmare was finally going to be dealt with. At least a part of it.

Chief Scheider was a tall, formidable looking man with milky-white skin, not like the cops you'd see on TV. His physique seemed better suited to a basketball player. But when he spoke, his voice was genial, warm. He extended his hand to Rian first, then to Jack. "Come in, have a seat. Would you like some coffee?"

"No, we're fine." Jack looked at Rian.

"I'll get right to it then. As Koontz told you, I'll be closing the Island. The team has already begun the pursuit. They outfitted barriers to keep the shark in the bay area. It's too large to leave the island now."

"I can't believe it's going so smoothly, I mean with closing the area down so quickly. No fights. No reluctance," Rian said.

Scheider chuckled. "Well, Mr. Woods was threatening to sue us if we didn't. It was kind of motivation enough. But I'm with you, Mrs. Field, as it is. So even if Jimmy hadn't been hurt, there's something too eerily coincidental about a Great White getting so close to shore, and not just once, but three times in a matter of weeks. It's uncanny."

Yes, she thought, uncanny was an appropriate word to describe it, though the Chief was ignorant of the deeper reasons for it. This wasn't a coincidence at all. Someone was out to hurt her. Yet she wondered about the veracity of that statement. If that were true, how did it explain Jimmy Woods's attack? She was more than troubled by the lack of an answer. She started to wonder if her senses were actually being determined by her PTSD, triggered by her flashbacks to that night. But how did that explain her uneasiness at certain times? She was growing frustrated. She had been so sure before. What had changed? She had to call Carly once they were through here.

"Mrs. Field?" The chief was staring at her.

She glanced over at Jack, who looked concerned. "What?"

"I said, we'll be posting notices that there is a Great White in these waters." He shook his head, as if troubled. "It just baffles me. We've been getting various reports about sightings in San Onofre State Beach, Dana Point, even Manhattan Beach, but here in Newport, it's just so out of the ordinary."

Rian almost believed that he was just as shaken as she was. "Well, the water has been hovering around sixty degrees, which is their preferred temperature." Somehow, though, that fact didn't comfort her.

"Yes, I suppose that makes sense. Do you have any questions for me?" he asked her.

"No."

He slapped his hands together, his lanky frame towering over them as he came around his desk to see them out. "I will be in touch with you before long with a status of our search. Take care."

Rian thought she had slept plenty in the past few days, with all the naps she'd taken, but when she and Jack stepped inside their home, she found herself drowsy and ready for sleep again. "I'm sorry."

"Rian, you don't need to apologize. Like Carly says, you have to take care of yourself. Remember you experienced this lack of energy sometimes after some of your other sessions."

She nodded and went to the bedroom and didn't remember falling asleep. She forgot about calling Carly. But this time, she did dream.

She found herself somewhere she had never been before. In the desert. But this was not an ordinary desert. It was a cold desert. Thick, clean snow spread across the vast, dry, weeded earth. In some areas, thin layers of ice had crystallized over the arms of cacti, which loomed over the barren ground like white ghosts. In other places, the snow lay in thick patches.

Instinctively, Rian knew that she was destined to encounter something here soon, a grave but imperative confrontation.

As she headed north, she found herself coming into close proximity to the mountains. The desert land fell flat across the earth in a strange sort of way. The mountains sat at an odd angle, leaning toward her as if they were about to collapse, so that it seemed like she was actually ascending through the valley. All around her, snow whipped up, down, swirling the air around like a film of white dust. She didn't know where she was going, but somehow she understood that she would soon find the answer.

As she continued "up", with the panoramic view of the mountains, a band of bears came galloping toward her. It was hard to tell if there were two or three of them because they ran so close together that they appeared to be one. She expected them to attack her, bite her, claw at her. Instead, they came to a halt and began to circle her as she continued her ascent. Though afraid, she kept her composure so that the bears could not detect how timid she really was.

To her surprise, the animals sniffed at her for several seconds and suddenly took off, rushing past her and disappearing into another dimension.

Rian walked faster, hoping to reach her destiny, even though she still remained unsure as to what that destiny was. Suddenly, she started to feel the eerie sensation that a perverse entity waited for her.

A cold wind swept up and closed around her as if to claim her as its property.

She reached the top of the desert; there was nowhere else to go. When she turned to look behind her, the snow had magically disintegrated.

Something dark rustled behind a nearby cactus. Seconds later, a black coyote emerged. It crept toward her and lowered its jaws as it growled deep in its throat. Its body was long and skinny, and its thick coat of fur had been shed as though it were not winter, leaving its body pale and sickly. But what was more notable than anything else were its glowing eyes.

She backed up slowly, terrified for her life. But then she realized that the coyote had no interest in her. In a single motion, it lunged into the air and tackled the bears.

Rian woke up in an icy sweat, terrified. She had dreams before, nightmares of being chased, of monsters like Freddy Krueger or Dracula, but this one had scared her far more than the others because something about it felt too realistic, too possible.

She looked over at Jack, who had fallen asleep. The clock on the nightstand read eleven o'clock. Through the window, the moon emitted a soft glow that cast a halo over Jack's head. She tugged on his sleeve. He moaned, clearly in a deep sleep.

She decided that talking to someone without Jack might give her a fuller picture. She had depended too much on him lately. For the first time in her life, she had found herself needing to receive solace and strength entirely through another human being. She needed to find a way back to autonomy. She thought of Hal.

Since losing his wife to cancer a few years ago, he had become quite the night owl. It was difficult to fall asleep without her, he'd told them. After making a quick phone call to Hal to confirm her visit and leaving Jack a note of her whereabouts, Rian grabbed her coat and purse and drove ten miles down the coast to Hal's condo.

They immediately fell into place like a couple of old friends. Hal brewed some coffee as she shared the news from the mayor, particularly the report of the shark and its massive dimensions. "It's probably a female. They are a bit larger than the male species. I just can't make sense of it being so close to shore. Twice it's come up to the pier. It isn't natural," she said as she sipped from her mug.

Hal reached over to gently squeezed her shoulder. "It might take some time, but we will figure this out." Then he sat back, pondering. "I'll be damned. I've been living in this town my whole life and I have never, ever, seen anything larger than a barracuda."

He rose from his steaming cup and began to pace, moving from the front door to the end of the kitchen counter and back to the front door as if trying to organize his scrambled thoughts. "This part of the ocean just doesn't cater to fish of greater size. That's what makes this place such a popular vacation spot. My friends been fishing in those waters for years and it's always been safe." He was talking as a man trying to convince himself of his own words.

Hal's house was situated a few feet from the water's edge, and Rian got up and walked with him over to the back window where they both stared out at the dark infinite mass of water, as if looking into the water would clarify the mystery. They stood that way for several moments until Hal broke the silence.

"Rian, darling, tell me what I can do right now. I can't stand to see you this way."

"You already are."

"I can't fathom this at all. Been a strangeness in the water." He shook his head. "Take care of yourself. We'll get those answers. It will take some time, but in my heart, I know we will."

She hoped he was right.

Chapter Eleven

~January 5 2016~

Rian and Jack spent a day at Newport Beach. Even though the beach was technically just three miles from Balboa Island where the incident had taken place, she felt protected. Away from the scene of the crime, as she had started to call it, she figured she'd be able to focus on enjoying herself and her husband. The beach was also the locale of peace that she had formed as the visual part of some of her mantras. They used to picnic here until the Institute started requiring more of her time. Her hope was that returning to this safe place and going through the motions of a normal and familiar activity would clear her thoughts and shed light on the meaning of the dreams.

The day was beautiful with the sun directly overhead shining down a soft warmth atop their skin. Three seagulls sailed about thirty feet above the ocean. They swooped down, unaware that anything might rise through the water, grab hold of their fragile bodies, and pull them down until they drowned.

A couple, just a few yards into the distance, rode on a jet ski, speedily skipping over the waves, never worrying that something monstrous could be lingering below them, its mouth probably wide open, ready to—

"Rian?"

She looked over at Jack, realizing that she had gotten tangled up in her own morbid world of imagination. She smiled meekly, but the lingering thoughts unsettled her. In order to get through this, she had to first dismiss these horrible ideas because if she allowed herself to favor these gross images, these mortifying possibilities, she knew she would buckle under them. Right now, strength needed to be her companion.

"I'll be fine. I'm just a little shaken. I'll be meeting with Carly in an hour, so that should help." But even as she said it, she was finding herself drawing further away from him.

When her dad died, just before they left their country cottage, her mom withdrew to such a degree that they ended up putting her in a home because she could no longer be reached. She and Rian had once been very close, but she could no longer turn to her. She visited her daily at first, but as the weeks passed her mother persisted in her lost world unable to recognize anyone and eventually losing the ability to speak. Rian and Jack had limited their visits to monthly. Even those lasted only five minutes. After all, what good did it do to talk to someone who had no memory of you and could no longer communicate?

At least her mom had done something years before those moments, something no one else had been able to do, given her a sense of victory. She'd forever be thankful for that. Sadly, though, she could no longer find that encouragement these days, and she found herself withdrawing more and more from Jack. The way her mom had withdrawn once Rian's father died, losing trust in others and in life itself. Was she right to think Jack would hurt her? Or was it just PTSD? And once more she realized that the attack on Jimmy Woods somehow threw a monkey wrench into her suspicions. For if someone were really after her, if this were personal at all, then how did Jimmy's attack fit into this?

She forced herself to focus on the beach activity. The shore itself was pitted with rows and rows of large pockets, like a sand-covered pool table. A group of kids were building a huge sand castle just far enough away from the tide. A young child was burying his daddy in the sand a few feet further down. The coastline was dotted with body surfers, toddlers squealing with delight, teenagers holding hands. Down below, a group of volunteers played in the ocean with members of the Special Olympics. It was enough to get Rian in the mood, to reach out and trust again, even if it lasted only temporarily.

She squeezed Jack's hand and dragged him down to the water. They giggled like kids as they scooped up broken sea shells. One shell in particular was opalescent inside and its beauty struck her in a special way. An ongoing breeze lifted the hair out of her face as much as it lifted her spirits. For a short time, she was able to feel a joyful singing in her heart.

Carly came downstairs to get her right away.

"Thank you for meeting with me. Some major things are happening with the shark attack. The Chief has sent out a team to find the shark."

"So this is good news. That means they identified the shark as the one who attacked the boy?"

"Yes."

"How does this make you feel?"

"Glad, but still uneasy."

"Uneasy about what?"

"I think that someone close to me was there that night in my home."

"Try to remember when you think this. What do you notice in your body?"

"It happens at any time, really, around anyone. My hands hurt sometimes. I've had headaches before. I don't even feel close to my husband a lot of the time, like I don't trust him. I don't know who to trust anymore and that scares me the most." She looked down at her hands that were clasped together tightly and how the strain of it blotched her fingers. "And I keep having nightmares. This one was about some bears that I thought were hunting me down until a coyote came in to attack them."

"What were you feeling in the dream?"

"Scared. Out of control. Like I couldn't escape."

"It may not directly allude to the events of that night, but the reaction you have is similar to what you felt then and it tells me that we need to continue the EMDR. This fear is a symptom of your PTSD."

"Could that also be behind my suspicion of people?"

Carly nodded. "It's normal to feel on edge at times. What is important is to notice when these sensations happen so that you can recognize them and concentrate on your safe place. I don't want to say that it's unreasonable to suppose that one of those men could be nearby, it's not, but I also don't want you to feel paranoid or to let the idea of it take over you."

They spent the last thirty minutes running through an EMDR session. This time she concentrated on a different aspect of that November time, focusing on their conversation. She wasn't able to make much out of anything they'd said because they had been extra careful to keep their voices down. But one word did come to her, a word she'd forgotten she'd ever heard. "Jack."

"Take a deep breath. Now, on a scale of one to ten."

"Ten."

"What were you thinking?"

"I could hear them talking, but the only thing I could make out was the word 'Jack'."

"OK. What do you think it means?"

She was scared now. "I don't know. The man, the one with the skeleton mask, said it like he was addressing the other man." She shook her head. "No, I can't. . . It can't be him."

"What did you notice in your body?"

"My heart going crazy and my stomach in a lot of pain. I was scared." She started crying. She didn't want to. She equated crying with losing control. But she couldn't fight it. She bent her head to see the tears falling onto the open palms of her hands like tiny raindrops. Vomit rose in her throat, but it quickly dropped to her stomach. "I'm sorry."

"Don't apologize. This happens a lot during EMDR. Some people get sick. Some cry. It's OK. Tell me about the mayor, the Chief's decision. How do you feel about this?"

"I'm relieved. I feel better. But not entirely. Like something that no one knows is being overlooked. And lately I feel like I'm withdrawing from Jack more than ever. And now this, this memory, that Jack might be involved. . ."

Carly instructed Rian through some relaxing exercises, starting with the top of her body to the tips of her toes as she drew in long breaths and exhaled them at each point of attention. After a few minutes, it was over, and the tension left her body.

***

He had intentions. Evil intentions. Never again would he succumb to the brutality and manipulation his father had used so well on him. He was learning new ways to cope, and nothing and nobody would stop him from reaching his goal—Complete Control.

He smiled at his reflection in the mirror. His eyes glinted with excitement, glossy and wide, eyes belonging to a predator. When he grinned, his white teeth flashed brightly. Perfect teeth. His two powerful hands clutched at each side of the sink. Veins bulged beneath the surface of his skin. Sweat glistened across his knuckles.

He lifted his left hand to his face and slowly put his fingers inside his mouth. He smiled as he bit down on them. Ohhh, how the taste of his own blood caused him to shiver. The blood gave him power.

He walked to his bedroom and peered out the window. Black puffy clouds rolled sensually across the darkening horizon. Thunder rumbled like the sound of tall buildings collapsing or a small bomb caressing the southern counties of California. The massive expanse overhead loomed more like a lair of hell rather than a peaceful sky as the dark clouds jetted across it, clawing at it like giant black fists.

He sighed with pleasure. He loved the night. It was the one time he felt truly himself. In the daylight, no one really respected him. Not even she had. All those self-centered, ignorant fools would one day give him the utmost respect. But it was *she* who would give it to him first. She owed him that.

As he stared outside, he waited anxiously for darkness to settle, like a small boy looking forward to unwrapping presents beneath the Christmas tree.

***

Rian watched with an unsettling feeling as the sky, frosty and cold, began to quickly darken behind clouds of black silk. A large fat drop of rain plopped onto her hand like the tears from moments ago. Suddenly, irrationally, she imagined herself beneath a sheath of poisoned clouds. She ran to her car.

In the safety of her car, she peered up through her window. New clouds were forming, tar-drenched masses that coiled like the movements of rattlesnakes while others transformed into vines that crawled as they cleaved to the sky. A soft rain began to descend across the windshield.

She picked up her cell phone and dialed Lilah. If anyone could dispel illogic or doubt, it would be her. She picked up on the first ring. "How are you?"

***

Black colored the sky like a great wing of a raven. Street lamps flickered on. Houses lit up like tiny candles underneath the blanket of night. He heaved a sigh of pleasure. At last, he could breathe freely again. Breathe without frustration or self-pity, without any of the weaknesses that preoccupied most humans. Night was his best friend. It embraced him and soothed his anxiety the way no mother or father could do. It cherished him, cradled him, loved him more than the most affectionate father. It adored him more than *she* had, powerful beyond a lover's gaze. The night brought fear to some people, worry over the day's troubles, but for him, the night gave him time to think, to plot. The night belonged to him.

***

Rian Field was a survivor. But lately she hadn't been tough enough to fight her own wars. For the first time in thirty-five years, she experienced absolute despair. She trusted that she would never again experience the bliss of her marriage or the safety she once knew. Even though it had been years since her father had died, she found herself resigning to despair. Death was closing in all around her. There was no use in fighting it. Gone was the joy she'd known when her father was still alive.

But something else was on her mind again. The shark. The team had been replaced weeks ago, but they still hadn't been able to catch it. As she watched Jack work in the kitchen, she didn't feel half of what she'd always felt for him, as if something had obliterated part of her feelings for him. But it wasn't this way only with Jack. Talking to Lilah on the phone felt strange too, like the level of familiarity had vanished, as if Lilah were a mere acquaintance. No, that wasn't quite it. More like Rian's ability to connect had been partially taken. And though she felt somewhat estranged from Jack, Rian couldn't be sure that it had nothing to do with anything he had done.

Jack was busy in the kitchen, so she dialed Lilah. She answered right away. "We're hoping that they catch the shark in the next few days. Therapy is helping me. I just feel so disconnected again, like before."

"What does Carly say?"

Rian opened her mouth to speak when an earthquake shook the house. The large window in the living room clattered violently. The couch began to ferociously vibrate as it if were being strangled by the grip of an enormous monster. A long jagged crack formed down the glass of the window, curved upward, jerked to the right, and spiraled down, created, it seemed, by a talon of that huge sea monster.

Jack was gripping the corners of the kitchen counter, his legs sprawled beneath the arch of the doorframe. Rian was frozen, the phone to her ear, as she watched doors swinging frantically, being pulled off their hinges and thrown down the hallway into the back part of the house. The chair she was sitting on shook with such violent force, she was certain it would shatter her limbs. Then the lights snapped off and the shaking came to a shuddering halt.

"Rian?!" Lilah shouted through the phone.

"We just had an earthquake," Rian found her voice, though it shook like the tremors of the quake. "Let me call you back."

The feeling of suspicion now turned to compassion for her husband. She hung up and ran to Jack, who was sprawled across the ground beside the refrigerator. "Jack?" He didn't move. She gently shook his arm. "Jack?"

He groaned and blinked his eyes opened. "Are you OK?"

Rian laughed. "I should be asking you that."

She helped him to his feet and they walked tiredly to the bedroom. When Rian neared the window, an overwhelming conviction took over again, that someone was going to shoot through the window. She hadn't experienced that in so many days, perhaps even a month, that it startled her. She pictured herself crumpled up on the carpet as waves of glittering confetti fell upon her. But then a different thought replaced the image, the hope that someone would shoot through the window, just to get it over with.

~The End of January 2016~

For the second time that week, Rian had an emergency session with Carly. This time, she told her about the powerful feeling that someone was out to get her and how every time she walked into their bedroom, she felt like someone would shoot through the window.

"I don't necessarily think it's one of the guys from that night. But the feeling is so powerful that it seems destined to happen. And I want it to happen. I just want to it to get over with so I can stop thinking it every time I walk by it."

"Part of the PTSD, it's called passive resignation." Carly went on to tell her to respond to those thoughts with something opposite, something that would make her feel protected, and to continue letting out the steam of thought and emotion and not to squash it.

Rian pondered the dreams from the last two nights and it made her wonder why she had forgotten them. Maybe she had "resigned" to those too.

"I had a dream, it's almost recurring, where someone kidnaps me and I get to the phone to call 9-1-1, but the cord has been pulled out of the wall, just like they really did, except I'm about to reconnect it but one of the men walks into the room. I got farther with this dream because in the ones from before the men never let me out of their sight. And this other dream, from last night, I did call the police and reported the crime, but the man put me on hold for another call."

"These sound like a good progression. Before, you were powerless, unable to get to the phone, but now you are actually making the call. How do you feel about the men in the dream?"

"I used to be scared, but now I can only focus on getting to the phone. It's almost like they aren't there." She paused, realizing that yet another dream had plagued her last night as well. "Then a man came to the door and asked, 'Whose turn to die?' The man next to me raised his hand and the guy shot him dead. The bullet knocked him to the ground on his back and he died instantly. The killer ran out and I followed him, but it was too dark outside. I called the cops, but they put me on hold. I found myself walking somewhere else and I saw this man who

I was sure was the killer but I didn't want him to know so I shook his hand and walked past him."

"Keep talking about these, tell Jack, so you can get them out. You don't want to hold these inside. I'd like you to try changing your routine at bedtime. Instead of going straight to your side of the bed, ahead of Jack, let him go in first or you both go in together. This will help you to respond differently to the window, and when you enter the bedroom tell yourself something that is the opposite of being shot at."

"Like I am safe?"

Carly nodded at her. As before, they ran through an EMDR session, Rian focusing on the scene where the skeleton-faced man had her pressed against the wall. She thought of fictional survivors. Chyna from Dean Koontz's *Intensity*, Laurie from *Halloween* and Sidney from the *Scream* films. She told herself she was out of danger, but she didn't believe that. Not entirely. After several seconds, Carly asked her what she felt, what she noticed. She repeated her thoughts.

"What do you think these obstacles are that are preventing you from feeling safe?"

"For the last few days, just like in the beginning when this all happened, I don't feel protected. I keep feeling like I don't have a future, that I'm going to die soon."

"Imagine a friend was thinking this. What advice would you give her?"

It was so hard to say the next words because she felt not just estranged from everyone in her life, but from God too, even though He had never really been anyone or anything important to her. Somehow, in ways she could no more understand than the link between the shark and that November night, He was starting to feel like more than just an abstract figure. "That God is right here."

"That's good. And when those feelings of death come, notice them and let them go. Get back in touch with reality. If you're outside, notice the sky is blue, people walking, the color of the grass. Or, if you're inside when these thoughts arrive, practice the Pattern Repetition Movement, patting your knees or crossing your arms over your chest and tapping your arms as you focus on a relaxing place."

"Why does it work?"

"When we're in our mother's womb, we detect her heart rate, which gives us that security of being safe, so that when you do a repetitive movement like rocking in a chair or playing the piano, and you're just focused on the rhythm of it, that feeling of being soothed is recalled."

Rian nodded, comforted by the simplicity of it. "But why do I feel so disconnected from everyone? It's like how my emotions weren't there when I first started therapy and how separate from me they were when talking about the break-in."

"You almost died that night and it has created this detachment from your life. Part of the PTSD, again, a way of coping." That made sense. "But we will continue working on it. You did wonderfully with the session today, and remember to keep practicing those techniques."

When she returned home, Jack was in the backyard playing with Champ, so Rian lied down on the couch for a quick nap, but when she tried to fall asleep, her heart started speeding madly like it was too scared to.

After they ate a late dinner, she and Jack went to bed. It was only eight o'clock, but she was exhausted from the EMDR. She had another dream. She was upset that she dream at all for it was as though she couldn't function without them. They were a reminder byproduct of the reality she could not seem to overcome.

This time, the dream was quick. She was handcuffed with a white sheet tied around her wrists and another one around her ankles. She was bound for several days until one day the makeshift shackles around her wrists loosened enough for her to kick them off. Quickly, she located a pair of scissors, and cut through the wrist bands, shouting, "I'm free!"

113

The next morning at breakfast, the dream lingered freshly in her mind. She shared it with Jack and he smiled at her. "Sounds like a good dream. Maybe it's your subconscious's way of telling you that you are free. Free from what they did."

"Yeah, maybe you're right." She smiled back and grabbed the toast as it popped up from the toaster.

The following week, she finished her last EMDR session and she no longer felt anxiety about the event. Maybe the dream was prophetic.

"You've processed a lot, Rian. We're done here. You are no longer feeling that jumpiness or having nightmares. But if something does come back, call me." Carly warmly shook her hand as she led her downstairs.

Chapter Twelve

"I think we should move," Jack said when Rian walked through the door. He was half-heartedly folding towels, moving in slow motion as if it hurt him to do anything. "You keep having these nightmares or you can't sleep or you feel like someone's going to hurt you. And I think if we just move and get away from this house you'll be able to recover sooner."

"I don't think that's the answer." She dropped her wallet on the counter and looked at Jack straight in the eyes. "I'm making progress with counseling. In fact, Carly said as long as I'm not experiencing jumpiness or those nightmares, I'm done with therapy."

She still felt like this was her home in spite of the personal violation against her, yet something more powerful motivated her—she refused to live in fear. No one was going to take her sense of self, much less her sense of comfort, away from her.

"Are you sure? It's not too hard to live here?"

"I feel like I need to be here still, at least for now." She wanted to add that she felt a strong undercurrent that was tossing her toward the culprits, on the way to some kind of crossing point, but a small part of her still wondered if he might be one of the offenders.

When they crawled under the covers, Jack attempted to touch her, but she turned away, so he went to sleep. She cried to herself because she didn't know how to feel close to him anymore.

In the decade of matrimony that they had shared, Rian had always desired him. In fact, she often found that she couldn't get enough of him, not just sexually, but emotionally as well. Now, in the darkness of their sanctuary, there might as well be an ocean between them, one filled with Great Whites.

The next day, Rian and Jack drove to the Institute together. Jack had some finishing touches to work on and Rian was teaching a class on marine tetrapods to a small group of local first graders.

Rian and Jack had tried for years, all ten years, to have children, but she had never been able to get pregnant, aside the one time, but she had quickly lost the baby. Thus, being around kids was bittersweet. The yearning to have kids had not entirely dissipated, but it had become tolerable enough for her to be around children. She was grateful, actually, to have a change in pace at work for it allowed her to take her mind off the shark and the previous incident and that energy into educating children. As she started her lecture, she found herself feeding off the excitement and the newness of the experience through which the kids observed her instruction.

"Now, should we start with mammals, sea turtles, or birds?"

"Birds!"

"OK, so let's take a look at some of these various species." She led them to a display of photographs with individual unmarked snapshots of various birds. "Tell me what you know about birds."

"They like to fly," said one girl.

"That's right. What else do you know?"

A small boy spoke up. "They like to go to the bathroom on your car." Everyone laughed.

"Well, what you may not know is that they are a very vulnerable species. What we do affects them too. So, it's important that we make good choices. For instance, birds eat twice their weight in food, so we can do our part by making sure to limit the use of toxins like pesticides or pollutants into the air."

Several kids had questions and comments as she went along in the lecture and for a good hour she found herself completely immersed in a pleasant world, one without lurking monsters.

When they broke for lunch, Randy and Shonda joined her and Jack for a picnic outside. Even though it was winter, the sun beat down at an eighty-degree temperature. For a change, the conversation focused on trivial topics, like the latest movies and trends until Rian turned it into a football talk-fest.

"My Steelers baby," Jack said proudly as he squeezed her arm.

"Six-time Super Bowl Champs," she said with pleasure.

"Dylan's not going to be too happy if his Colts lose to them tomorrow tonight," Shonda said.

Randy was in a serious mood, and what he said next interrupted the light-hearted humor. "What's happening with the team Koontz has out? Are they getting anywhere?"

Jack shook his head at Randy to silence him and Randy looked pissed. Rian stopped eating her sandwich, wondering what was happening. She had never seen tension like this between them. There was a dark edge in Randy's voice as he said, "OK, Jack, have it your way." He picked up his fork, like he was going to use it for something murderous, and everyone looked at him with held breath until he stabbed his salad with it instead.

When they finished eating, Rian thought the weirdness was over. But somehow the heat increased and it scorched the parking structure, the grass, their faces. Unfortunately, that fire sought its way inside Jack and Randy, and the picnic area soon became a battlefield. It started out slowly, stealthily. Randy turned into a snake, shedding his former self that she liked so well and becoming an evil predator with Jack as his quarry. Randy's brown eyes turned a flaring black, his mouth opened slightly and out came a hissing sound as he spit on Jack. "You have a wonderful wife who has been nothing but loyal to you. And here you are, acting so high and righteous up on your temple like no one can ever beat you, you damn hotshot Marine. You are not this innocent guy like you want everyone to believe. So tell the truth and set her free." Randy rose from his knees and moved toward Jack, his fingers gnarled and his teeth set straight like the shark's when it came at her from under the water.

Jack had risen too, but he was calm and composed, undeterred by Randy's sudden and strange and uncharacteristic lashing out. His green eyes flickered with preparation. He was always, as a Marine, ready for anything. He had to be.

Shonda looked around nervously and Rian could see that she was trembling, but Rian wasn't willing to move because she didn't know what might happen to her or to Jack if she did. She kept her gaze on the two men, not knowing who to trust and wondering which one of them she actually knew.

"I think it's time for you to leave. I'll let Westen know you're not feeling well," Jack told Randy. He amazed Rian, the way that someone could tear him down, threaten him, and yet he could take it and not back down. It is one of the qualities she admired about him. But what did Randy mean when he said that Jack should tell the truth? She tried searching for an answer in Jack's eyes, but he was totally focused on Randy.

"I will tear you up." Randy's knuckles furled, flexed, and tightened.

Jack continued to stare him down.

As if waking from a dream and realizing where he was, Randy's hands went lax and he looked at her, then Shonda, with soft brown eyes. "I better go," he softly said.

The rest of the afternoon Rian found working with the school kids difficult, though her mood managed to change for the better once they started talking about mammals. One little girl in particular had some jokes to share. She was a dark-haired beauty who had been quiet the entire day, until now. Rian found herself laughing out loud and she nearly forgot about the altercation at lunch.

Jack spent most of his afternoon going over plans with Westen. Dylan swung by to pick up Shonda shortly thereafter. Rian had to wait almost an hour until Jack was ready to go.

The ride home was quiet. When they got there, Jack poured himself a shot of whiskey. Champ rubbed his nose against his owner's arm and Jack patted his head. Rian fell onto the couch.

"What was that all about with Randy today?" She looked over at Jack whose face was flushed from the liquor. He was clutching the edges of the bar as if the bar itself was keeping him grounded. His eyes didn't meet hers right away for he was contemplating something. When he did respond, his voice came from far away.

"I don't know." He poured himself another shot, downed it, and grabbed the bar again. Looking straight at her, he said, "I have no idea."

The next day, Rian turned on the TV to watch the game. The first quarter was coming to a close and the Steelers were behind. Usually, Rian would be a little annoyed, but she didn't feel much of anything. Not about that. All of her emotions were concentrated in one area—Jack.

He had gotten up early to take care of some last touches at work and while he was gone, Rian realized how horribly wrong everything was. Last night, in bed, she kept as far away from him as possible because their conversation had been ambiguous. Why had he thought about her question before he answered it? What could he possibly need to contemplate? It left her wondering about him. Was he being forthright? Honest?

She watched the sporadic colors on the screen as they wildly flashed across the screen, mesmerized by the erratic motion. "I don't know" and "I have no idea", those same words came to her now in answer to her speculation. She didn't even call Lilah to confide in her. At this point, she couldn't straighten everything out in her own head, much less attempt to relay it someone else.

The Steelers were back on. It was the second quarter. They were still losing. Jack made some phone calls to all of their friends, inviting them over for the game, but only Floyd, Sean and Kristen would be able to make it.

She got up, went to the kitchen, and made herself a bacon, lettuce, and tomato sandwich with dill pickles on the side, and a tall glass of chocolate milk. It was her favorite meal, a bit quirky according to all of their friends, but nevertheless her favorite. With the sound of football in the background and the house all to herself, Rian experienced a peace of mind that for the last two years remained more of a remote awareness. She smiled as she chewed on the bacon.

On the television, the Steelers place kicker attempted a field goal and missed. Normally, she would have gotten a bit worked up, jumping up and down in disappointment, but she was in good spirits now and she simply shrugged and took a sip of the milk as she nudged a barstool up to the counter.

When she sat down, the walls started to rattle. She turned to face the glass door that led out into the backyard. Next to it was a maple-framed photo holding the United States flag and the Marine Corp flag. The glass panel began to shutter, making the flags wave.

Another earthquake.

She scooted her butt off the bar stool and inched her way over to the doorway that connected the kitchen to the dining area. Behind her, the routine sounds of the game faded and were replaced by a strange warbling. Frowning, she slowly turned to face the TV. A rainbow of squiggly lines jumped erratically across its face as the electronic gibberish turned into a quavering melody. She froze, the muscles of her heart becoming strangely twisted as her ears adjusted to the odd musicality that was sifting through the sound waves. To her left, a thumping noise split the air and reverberated across the living room, tore into the kitchen, and then came to a halt at the edge of the doorframe under which she remained standing. As she looked down, she noticed that her knees were shaking and her hands were clasped together into a knot.

Abruptly, the TV snapped off. The shaking stopped. The peculiar music ceased. All was still. She held her breath, anticipating the next surprise.

Through the glass-paned doors, the casita was visible. Next to it, a red robin alighted on the small angel water fountain that Dylan and Shonda gave to them as a housewarming gift. Rian liked birds, particularly red robins, but in that moment its crimson body only made her think of blood, and she shivered.

The front door was about ten feet behind her. From that direction there came a hollow but very distinct utterance. "Rian."

She whirled to face the door. No one there. She stared hard at it for several minutes, waiting for her name to be spoken again, but all she heard was silence. Then it happened.

An object crashed through the back doors, blowing out the glass encasement and producing an odd symphonic blast of clattering noise that resembled something like a cluster of chimes crashing into each other as shards of glass blew apart over the marble coffee table, ripped into the leather couch, and splattered across the acacia floorboards.

Rian broke free from her standing position in the doorway and ran faster than she ever had, down the hallway to the bedroom where she slammed the door so hard that it shook in its frame and sent a picture of her and Jack tumbling from the nightstand to the carpet.

She quickly locked the door and hurried to the far end of the cherry wood dresser that sat next to the door. Putting all of her weight into it, she pushed with her back against it, digging her feet into the carpet as she pressed her body into the heavy piece of furniture. The dresser slowly budged closer to the door, frustratingly slow, but she continued to push nonetheless as if her life depended on it. *Because* her life depended on it. The dresser was halfway across the door now. She shoved harder until the muscles in her back grew tender. The dresser filled the entire span of the door. Her breathing came rapidly and she placed her palms against her knees as she tried to take in air.

This was it. She was going to die. For the past two years, she had been highly aware of mortality nudging her and constantly reminding her that her day was coming. It had finally come. It was her turn to die.

"Rian?"

She stood erect, held her breath. Was it the voice from a few minutes ago?

"Are you back there?" Whoever it was sounded far away, maybe in the kitchen. It was a male voice, not quite familiar to her at first, not quite real. She recalled the vibrating walls and the strange symphony of TV noise and shattering glass and the single utterance of her name, and she wondered what was going on.

"It's me. Floyd." He was closer, just a few feet away. The doorknob rattled. "What happened? Rian, are you in there?"

She exhaled. "Hold on." She pushed the dresser out of the way and unlocked the door.

Floyd was standing in the doorway, his feet spread apart and his arms tense at his sides as if waiting for an attack.

"What's going on?" He glanced down the hallway toward the tangled mess.

"I have no idea. I thought there was an earthquake happening until someone threw something through the back door." She peered around the doorframe as if the answer might be waiting in the hallway.

"Jack called me and said to come on over for the game. He said everyone was going to be here, but I'm the only one here."

She looked at him. "How did you get in?"

"When no one answered the front door, I went around the back way to see if you guys were in the living room and that's when I saw the mess."

Floyd followed her back to the living room. Bits of glass were sprinkled across the floor, glittering like a broken mass of forgotten jewels. She took a reluctant step toward the couch and stopped. Just inches from the marble coffee table a heavy metal anchor rested. The anchor that belonged to *Freedom*.

"What the hell?" Floyd asked. He stooped to examine the chaos as Rian carefully sidestepped bits of jagged glass.

"Someone tried to kill me.

Floyd rose to face her. "I'll call 9-1-1. You call Jack." He gently touched her shoulder and squeezed before getting out his cell phone. The Emergency Dispatch was fast and the police arrived in two minutes.

Unexpectedly, she experienced the uncanny sensation of two years ago. The pending doom, the certainty that life was over, and the reality that she would never see Jack again all came pouring into her right then. Oh, sure, it made sense because both occasions had taken place in this house, but it wasn't just that fact alone. She was entirely positive that the two events were tied together and, ultimately, a part of the shark attacks too.

One of the detectives looked for prints on the anchor, but whoever had handled it had been smart enough to wear gloves. But because no one actually entered the premises, the police could do nothing more.

"Rian!" Jack entered the room and embraced her. She let him, falling with relief into his arms. "What happened?" He looked at Floyd for an answer.

"I got here right after it happened. Someone threw your boat anchor through the door, but that's all I know." He threw a calculated look over to Jack and Rian wondered what it meant, but before she had time to question it, Sean and Kristen appeared at the front door.

Kristen, usually keyed up with a smile on her face, looked worried as she approached them. "Rian, are you OK?" She glimpsed the chaos of the room.

"Yeah. No one got in, just someone trying to scare me." She hugged Kristen, feeling a little bit safer. Kristen was looking at her with concern as Sean engaged in quiet conversation with Jack and Floyd. Again, the unsettling feeling that someone here was out to hurt her returned fully. Whoever it was knew her, had been there that night, and was here again to remind her of it.

Rian excused herself from the group, her shoe crunching on a small piece of glass as she made her way back to the bedroom.

"Rian?" Jack called after her, but she kept moving.

She fell upon the bed and heard Jack behind her. "Ask them to go. Please," she begged.

"I already have. I could tell you wanted to be alone." He knelt beside the bed and stroked her hair.

"It's the same person, I just know it, and since he doesn't have any record to speak of, any fingerprints in the system, nothing will happen."

He kissed her forehead, her lips. "Shh. Don't talk like that. We don't know anything for sure. We have to think positive thoughts. Try to rest. I'm going to go clean up."

She didn't know if Jack could be trusted, but what choice did she have? "Who won?"

He turned in the doorway and grinned. "Steelers."

After a little while, Jack came back into the room. "Floyd called. He says he's coming back over with some news about the search team. Apparently, he's editing the story."

"Oh." She didn't know what to say to that. It was a story she had been waiting to hear for nearly a month, but to actually learn something about it brought about a new emotion. Fear. Fear that the shark had been spotted, but was unattainable. Or that the Chief had retracted his orders and that no team had gone out because they had come to the conclusion that Rian Field was crazy and that this talk about shark sightings had been merely her imagination, or that the Sundancer had collided with some anchor or waterline or something and that little Jimmy Woods's attack had been nothing more than an isolated incident. If any of these outcomes were true, Rian feared something even greater—that she would lose her mind.

"Rian?" It was Jack standing before her, his face so close to hers that she could feel his breath brushing against her neck. He had taken a hold of her shoulders and was watching her with a face of worry.

Someone knocked on the door. Jack released her and went to answer it. Rian followed him. Floyd looked at them with eyes bright and welcoming as though he carried nothing but good news to share. Or was it just a face to appease her and the real news would reveal what she'd dreaded to hear? They sat down in the living room, Jack and Rian on the couch next to where the broken glass had been and Floyd sitting diagonal in the brown leather love seat. Floyd was brushing his hands together as if he were dusting away some kind of dirt or stain. He glanced at Jack, then Rian. "The team has been searching day and night every day this week. It's been long and exhausting for them, so they took today off, but they will be back in the water first thing in the morning. They have gotten close to what they believe might be the shark."

He was just doing his job, she knew that, but the vexation probed her as it had before. "What does that even mean?"

"There have been several sightings of dorsal fins, some turning out to be dolphins, others bigger fish, possibly the Great White that. . .".

"So, it's a poker game."

"What do you mean?"

"They're gambling and hoping to win. It's a toss-up, an anything-can-happen deal, heads or tails flip of the coin, a roll

125

of the dice." She sighed and picked up a microscopic piece of glass that had been missed, hidden underneath the edge of the couch. "They will never find him this way." The glass sparkled like a diamond in the palm of her hand like a deceptive stone. Rian didn't want to be hopeful about the situation because she didn't know if she could bear to be let down. She knew that she was being pessimistic, perhaps even unfair to Floyd. After all, he was just doing his job. "What are you going to write?"

"Essentially that the team is continuing their search with the optimism that they are getting closer to tracking the shark."

Rian turned away and stared out the back door, the door through which someone had invaded their home. Over two years ago she had been violated when two masked men entered the front door by force, and though this time no one actually harmed her, she felt an identical feeling of violation return to her, that same sense of the uncanny. That overpowering conviction that both incidents shared a connection.

Three days later, Floyd dropped by unexpectedly. Both Jack and Rian were working in the garage; she didn't expect to hear what Floyd said next.

"The team was out on the ocean, within feet of the shark. They were able to tag it, but things got wildly out of their control, someone fell overboard and the other two were attacked by the shark when it smashed into the side of the vessel. In fact, there was a recording. They set up equipment to keep audio and video running during their expedition. The recording shows that the shark managed to pin itself to the floorboards, blocking their way out, and as a result keeping them pinned down as the water built up and covered their bodies."

"Oh my God," she said.

"This is not public information yet, so I need you to keep quiet on the details. The report of their death will be aired later tonight in a TV news release, but that's all they'll know at this point. An investigation needs to be conducted first."

"And the shark?"

Floyd looked surprised. "I don't know. I think it may be out of the area now."

The room felt stuffy to her. She needed fresh air. Without explaining, she excused herself from the room. Jack followed her out of the garage, watching her as she got into the car.

"Where are you going? You don't just leave. Not like that."

She took a breath, shoved the key into the ignition, and glanced up at him. Deep worry was in his eyes. "You're right. I'm sorry. This whole thing has just become too much."

"Do you want to go back to Carly?"

"You know, every time you bring therapy up it sounds like a threat."

He knelt down so that their faces aligned. "No," he said softly. "That's not what I mean to come off like at all. I just want my wife back."

She smiled and gripped the steering wheel. She turned the key and the engine revved, changing the somber tone into one of desperation. She didn't know where she was going, just somewhere. Anywhere but here. She looked at him again and saw the love in his face, and she thought she could trust it. After all, it looked like the same face she had seen almost every day for the past ten years. But she didn't know if she could. In fact, she didn't know who was being truthful. That thought just about did her in. She was also starting to wonder if she was reading too much into everything he did. Not just Jack, but Floyd, Dylan, Randy, and Sean. She had to go or she would just stay in this house and let these tangled thoughts take over her until she was a pathetic mental blob curled up in the middle of their bed. She refused to let herself become that way.

"I'll be back soon," she told him and managed to kiss him on the lips before backing out of the driveway.

Chapter Thirteen

The freeways were busy due to rush hour so Rian took the side streets. She didn't really know where she was going. It was already dark outside, the street lamps barely illuminating the sidewalks as she maneuvered through the bordering neighborhoods. Most people were either driving home or already at home so very few people were walking around outside.

A lone dog trotted down the sidewalk in the same direction she drove, as if keeping pace with her. It reminded her of Champ and she regretted how little time she had devoted to him lately. The strangeness of the events and the certainty that someone was out to hurt her, someone close, had taken such a solid hold of her to the point that she had forgotten the important things in life. Like spending quality time with Jack and Champ.

Within a month after she'd been held prisoner, they purchased him when he was just eight weeks old. In the beginning, the three of them spent nearly every evening eating dinner together, Jack and Rian at the kitchenette and Champ at his silver bowl next to their feet. The ritual was always followed by a plate of desserts for Jack and her, and a special beefy biscuit for Champ. As a rule, she and Jack would play a board game, usually Monopoly, which Jack always won, while their pup chewed on a squeaky toy to his heart's delight. They would follow the game with a movie, typically an action flick as they soon discovered that the genre turned out be a favorite for all three of them. Jack tried several different types of movies—horror, comedy, drama, romance, science fiction, thriller, but none of them had delighted Champ the way action films did. He grew easily bored with any other type of movie, usually moaning or closing his eyes to express his boredom, but the instant that an action movie was popped into the player, his golden ears perked up and his head would cock just slightly as he stayed his eyes on the screen.

The Golden's favorite movies, they quickly found, were those involving Jackie Chan. Apparently, not only did Champ appreciate a good fight, he liked his fights to be fun too, and Mr. Chan certainly added a unique sense of humor to his stunts.

She drove out of the residential area and turned right onto a main street. Crimson light washed over her face as she passed under a stoplight. A tear fell across her nose as she regretted how little attention she'd given to her boys and when she looked in the rearview mirror it looked like a tear of blood. She had never really cared to think about God, but now she said a silent prayer. Oh God, how she missed the past, before that nearly fatal night.

The traffic started to loosen up as she passed shopping centers, a park, fast food restaurants. She felt like she was just wandering around town like the way her mind wandered now, full of disorder and erratic pathways that led to the same destination—nowhere.

But then she remembered the fish. Fortunately, the pet store had late hours throughout the week and within five minutes she was pulling into the parking lot. The same young woman, Trina, helped her again. She remembered Rian. "So nice to see you. Do you think you will be taking home a fish this time?"

"Yes."

"Is your friend with you?"

"No, just me."

"Well, let me know if you need any information about our selection." She flashed a smile and spun around to assist another customer.

Rian walked over to the rows of aquariums to revisit the various types of fish, and just as before, they all fascinated her, making it difficult to decide on a type of fish. As she moved from one tank to the next, her heart tickled her as she rediscovered a childlike joy in her that she thought had been completely lost. The various colors of the fish, the gleaming movements, and the dashing and colorful motions took her breath away. But her body started to shake and she couldn't quite make out why. She peered behind the tanks, searching for someone lingering in the shadows, but detected no one. What was it that was making her sweat and shake? Her eyes caught on the fluid darting of golden fish. Fish. The shark. She had to get out of there.

She hurried down to the Institute to meet with Shonda, who was a part of the replacement team to track down the Great White, though she worked only behind the scenes. She was busy in the lab, bent over a table, sequencing DNA, but she immediately stopped her work and came over to Rian.

In the last month, according to Shonda, the team had tried a new strategy and put into place a different kind of tag, satellite tags on some of the sharks. It was feasible that those marked fish would come into contact with *the* fish. "We've been pretty busy in the past few weeks and it has been so long since I have heard anything that I nearly forget about the research the team's been doing. It can sometimes be pretty dull as there are usually inconsequential movements detected from marine animals. Sorry, Rian, there's nothing new to report."

"So tell me what else you got going on," she responded, trying not to sound disappointed.

"The Institute has partnered with other facilities in tracking other types of sharks to study how they communicate. There are very long periods of waiting in between sightings. Still, it is fascinating to us each time a shark surfaces because it allows us to track their location."

Rian wasn't privy to the experimentation and she had little knowledge of the recent changes in technology when it came to tracking fish, mostly by choice, so she found the information Shonda was relaying to be quite interesting. "How do you guys do it?"

"Electronically. We attach a satellite tag to the dorsal fin so that whenever it breaks the surface of the ocean, the device sends out a signal radio signal to a receiver. These tags are set to a timer and they transmit any motion that is detected, be it a change in water temperature or depth. They combine sounds and transmission to a receiver in a single device allowing us to monitor the frequency of shark interaction too but more importantly helping us determine where they encounter one another so that we can improve their conservation. Imagine how much more effective our class dives will be with the increase in shark sightings!"

"That sounds fascinating."

"You really should come on board, I mean literally too. The expeditions are so amazing and we have frequent opportunities with the classes that we're running. There's been a major influx of upper elementary kids lately, making these types of excursions more and more available, which gives us ample opportunity to increase our current knowledge of marine life interaction." Shonda busied herself with something at the table and Rian nodded as her mind began to churn.

"How far do they travel on a daily basis?"

"Our research shows that they journey at least forty-three miles a day. And we've known for some time now that they either like to stay pretty close to the surface, within fifteen feet of it, or they prefer to dive deep, approximately 1,000 to 1,500 feet down."

Rian knew these particular facts already, but it still fascinated her. Even though she hadn't been directly involved in the actual navigations, she remembered the studies done by many outside research teams over the past decade or two. She had hoped in the time she'd spent working here that some of that fear, that fear of physically swimming with the sharks, would subside. It hadn't.

The memories of her father's last minutes came to her. The heart attack had overpowered his will to live and she, with her mom by her side, watched as the light faded from his spirit. His eyes had watered, pools of tears contained in his soft blue eyes, a look of devastation and confusion entering them as he gasped for one last breath of air.

And now something else had taken over her, something that overpowered even the fear. Determination. If she was going to overcome the paralysis that had controlled her in the past, if she was going to create a new future for herself, one with freedom, then she was going to have to break the heavy chains of timidity that had held her down. She was going to have to fight.

"I need to go, Shonda. Thank you for everything."

"Rian, what can I do?"

She shook her head hopelessly.

"Are Jack and Randy on speaking terms?" she asked Rian.

"They haven't spoken since the picnic. I still don't know what that was all about. Well, I have to go." She hugged her.

A week went by, and the more Rian found herself at work, the more she felt compelled to do something about the shark. She couldn't stop thinking about it swimming around out there waiting for its next prey. Koontz and the Chief had remained silent about the former team. The news, as Floyd informed them, simply announced the team's deaths but had yet to go into detail. The Chief had already begun an investigation, but she wondered why a video recording wasn't enough. She was tired of waiting for the latest team to track it. She had to take this into her own hands. But it needed to be under the radar, which meant she couldn't tell anyone, not even Jack, because she knew they would try to stop her, or at the very least, worry over her. She didn't want anyone worrying. This was just something she had to do, and it would be easier and more efficiently executed if no one got in her way.

Surprisingly, in that week, Jack made up with Randy and the two of them went to the Steeler's game out at Qualcomm Stadium, where they were competing in the playoffs against the San Diego Chargers. Since it was an afternoon game, they wouldn't be back for several hours, which gave her plenty of time to carry out her mission.

In Balboa Island, the morning was cool. A morning fog curled across the water. Yellow police caution tape was strewn across the length of the walkway. She ducked underneath it. *Freedom* had been repaired, and as soon as she stepped into it, her eyes warily watched the lapping water.

Rain from the week before had lasted several days, bringing colder weather and a freshness to the air.

Five weeks had passed since she'd last been in the Sundancer. In that time, Jack had a new anchor refitted and the body damage from the shark attack repaired. As soon as she stepped into the boat, she was reminded too much of her last journey and she thought it might impede her from fully pursuing the shark. The muscles in her neck and back tensed. If she were going to be able to go through this, she would have to get used to the water again, no matter how difficult or uncomfortable it might be. That newfound determination soon overrode the tension. Dressed in her diving gear, she plunged into the water.

She spent some time below, noticing nothing spectacular, just the expected seaweed and rocks. The tightness in her muscles alleviated after several minutes and she slowly escalated toward the surface of the Pacific Ocean. Bubbles evaporated quickly into the salt water. She pumped her legs as if riding a bicycle and gently exhaled into her scuba mask. Seconds later, she emerged from the wet abyss.

She had explored underwater for around fifteen minutes, so her body had adjusted to a warmer temperature in the scuba gear. After she climbed into the cockpit, she removed the mask. A blast of sea air hit her like a cold slap and rushed into her lungs. As she peeled off the rubber suit, the soft ocean breeze, smelling of sand and seaweed, tickled her face. The breeze was in constant motion here and it cooled her neck where the sun was already beating down. The salty wind tossed her strawberry blonde hair all over her face until she pulled it back into a ponytail.

Her heart was beating crazy fast beneath her suit in a nervous and exhilarated tempo. The whole time she'd been underwater, she had been plagued by the thought of the shark creeping up behind her and suddenly appearing from behind a plankton. Now in the cockpit, she was expecting to be knocked out of the boat and, thus, forced to deal directly with the shark in a physically close countdown. She looked out at the massive face of the Pacific as it tossed its aquamarine waves toward the shore and dissolved into a dark sapphire glass sheet miles into the horizon.

Underneath the diving apparatus, she wore a short-sleeved T-shirt and black nylon tights. From underneath the driver's seat, she withdrew an over-sized gray sweatshirt and pulled it over her head.

She was getting hungry. Shonda and Dylan had agreed to meet her for lunch at one of Balboa Island's restaurants. Afterward, she would venture back into the ocean, this time staying in the boat.

But she wasn't just here to find the shark. She had to get over her fear of the ocean, that ironic truth that Jack always teased her about. What kind of person pursued a degree in Marine Biology, but was scared of the ocean? It was the mystery of the fish that fascinated her. Life, itself, was a mystery. The makeup of Great Whites eluded scientists for years. They could only see fifty feet ahead, so they relied on their sense of smell to seek out prey. They could detect blood up to three miles away. They could swim up to fifteen miles per hour. All the basic facts were known, but they still mystified humans. So here she was, anticipating answers that would fill the missing pieces of her own life story.

She slipped on her tennis shoes and reached inside the compartment between the passenger and driver seats, grasping the set of keys to the boat. She looked around her and found herself all alone in this great body of water, just like that night a few weeks ago. Only this time, she was saturated with dread, further cemented by the posted sign that warned about a Great White in these waters. The waves were calm, quietly lapping against the boat, but it was a deceiving lull.

She tucked the towel underneath her arm.

Ten minutes later, she met Dylan and Shonda ate a local bakery where they all enjoyed sandwiches and coffee. Shonda shared more news about her findings in the lab and something about a grant for more research. After an hour or so of chatting, the two took off and Rian strolled over to the pier.

The pier was over 1,000 feet long. Rian stood at the end of it, near the diner, observing the afternoon crowd. At least five people had thrown their fishing lines into the water, patiently chatting as they awaited a bite. She spent several minutes gazing at the dark waves as they rolled toward shore. Seagulls cried out to each other as they circled overhead, their wings gliding effortlessly in symphony. A few feet to her right, an old man laughed with delight as his toddler grandson attempted to chase down a seagull that perched itself atop the railing of the pier. Two teenaged boys were playfully wrestling at the end of the walk. A mother and her two children were talking animatedly as they pointed to the swells of the deep.

When she returned to her towel, she dipped her feet into the sand, the warm velvet touch of the fine pebbles sticking to the contours of her skin. She had been to this very spot on many occasions with Jack and it had always signified a place of happiness and relaxation. Yet, as she lied on her back, a soft breeze that fluttered against her face seemed to purport some kind of warning. Then came the feeling, once again, that her life was nearing peril, that someone was observing her from close by, though not close enough to be detected.

She sat up and looked straight ahead at the water. People continued to play freely as if imminent danger was nowhere in sight. She let her eyes travel down the coast, to the pier, where a small handful of kids were frolicking. To the left, down the shoreline, sunbathers rubbed lotion on each other or had fallen asleep, contentment across their faces. But not fear. To the right, a large crowd formed alongside a volleyball net, cheering on their favorite team, smiles and laughter upon their faces, but nothing indicating the least sense of dread.

No one here was plagued with the belief that their life might be threatened any minute, not by a shark and certainly not by some masked stranger. Rian envied them. Gone was any feeling of contentment or security. She knew better than to believe in such a hoax. Whoever said ignorance was bliss was a fool because what you didn't know could hurt you. Today that ignorance would be turned into an understanding. The mystery of the masked men would no longer elude her. She didn't know why she was so certain of this, just that she was. She knew that their identity would be discovered and that she would be set free from the dark domain she'd been living under ever since.

Life was a mystery. Like anyone else, she couldn't anticipate its next move, but from here on out she would at least be prepared to withstand and overcome any surprise.

She lied back down. As a small spray of ocean water kissed her face, she closed her eyes and took in a deep breath of the salty air. Her muscles were no longer taut, her mind no longer clouded. She was ready to face whatever waited for her in that water. And for whoever stood behind the shadows.

When she opened her eyes, she realized she must have fallen asleep on the beach longer than she'd thought because the sun was already initiating its descent for the night. Rolling up the towel, she shook the sand off her shoes, drove back to her boat, and donned her rubber suit in a single motion. The sounds of the beach faded until all she could hear was the splashing of the waves against the dock.

Because the sensing equipment that tracked the shark's tag was located on a home computer at the Institute, she realized that the only way she could track it anonymously was to look for it. Yet, she wasn't defenseless. She had come prepared, having brought two weapons. After spending hours of research considering the different and most effective methods for protecting herself, she decided first on her KA-BAR, for its double-edged blade, hoping that a swift stab would take care of most of the dirty work and if not, she would use a bangstick, essentially a pole which came mounted on a 26" rod and ball assembly. A stainless steel chamber housed a live round of ammunition with a ready firing hairpin, a safety feature that delayed the projectile until she was ready to set it off.

She looked out at the silent waves rocking back and forth across the dark blue surface and it seemed impossible that anything was lurking below. But she knew better. It was waiting for her. Her heart started rattling in its cage and she looked down to see her hands trembling.

She watched the sun disappear from sight, leaving behind a rosy hue that stained the sky, and that soon faded into a deep black.

After securing everything in the storage box near the aft of the boat, she inserted the key into the ignition. The motor droned loudly and vibrated to life. That's why she didn't hear the splash when a large dark fin pulled up through the water.

She threw herself to the floor of the boat, tackled open the storage box, wrapped her right hand around the KA-Bar, and swung around to face the beast.

The shark's mouth was wide as water sprayed upward from its second thrust into the side of the boat. The scar she left on its face last November from the KA-BAR shined brightly.

Rian's breathing came in large shallow gasps, the air tasting strangely dry as she tried to whet the knife. She raised her right arm into the air and sunk all eight inches of the blade into the shark's skull. The creature's eyes rolled back. Its massive body descended into the water.

Rian stumbled back to the driver's seat, keeping her eyes on the water. Several seconds passed. Minutes. And then a shiny fin poked through the water, just feet away from the boat. The knife gleamed from its head like a hellish nightmare.

She stooped to the bottom of the boat and grabbed the bangstick. Unscrewing the cap off a bottle of nail polish, she went to work waterproofing the primer. If she used enough force, the projectile—the .357 Magnum caliber—would hit the fish. But she had to do it just right.

The fin rose higher.

She removed the firing pin, aiming the weapon at a linear angle, and gave a firm quick thrust at the shark's belly, inches below the water's cap. BOOM! The sound of the projectile exiting reverberated in the air around her as the projectile exploded underwater.

The shark had no intention of giving up. Its massive body pushed upward through the swelling waves and it thrashed and jerked, trying to free itself of the bullet.

Rian dropped the bangstick to the floor. This wasn't going to work. She had only one last resort. She hoped to God it would work. It had to. It took her less than thirty seconds to lasso the rope, but it felt like minutes, too much time. The amateur-fashioned cord hung several feet down, fastened to the stainless steel ski tow eye. The shark was still thrashing about just two feet away, its glossy fin tossing side to side, desperate to rid itself of the pain.

Then it disappeared underwater. She lowered the rope inches above the surface of the ocean. Several minutes passed and Rian began to worry that the fish had vacated the area for the night. The waves subsided as did the light of the sun. Only a soft glow from the resurrected moon sparkled across the face of the deep. Ten minutes went by. She winched the rope back onto the boat. All was eerily still until the face from her nightmare stabbed through the water, its fangs gleaming as its mouth opened wide. Maybe twenty feet separated them, but the gap was closing fast. She clutched the rope so tight that her hands burned.

Ten feet away.

She dipped the rope back over the ocean. The shark jerked right so that its body ran parallel to the boat's. Its massive snout pushed up in a perpendicular motion and the fish plunged through the noose. The rope glazed around its enormous head and around its horrible jaws, and just as it was about to reach its dorsal fin, she seized the rope with both hands and squeezed the noose tight.

The minutes ticked by quickly. The fish stopped thrashing, its face buried in the water, its fin slack in the unforeseen trap, its body drifting uselessly.

Five minutes later, it was dead.

Rian realized that her stomach had been twisted in knots, her shoulders taut, her hands curled stiffly, because as soon as the shark stopped breathing, her body sagged to the floor with relief.

She phoned the police department first from her cell phone, then Jack. Chief Scheider arrived with some of his deputies ten minutes later. Jack arrived a few moments after that. The Chief contacted Koontz and he followed immediately behind Jack. Jack hugged her tightly.

Three deputies tossed a large net into the water to start the process of lifting the shark onto the walkway. Jack's hug made her realize how long it had been since she'd felt that close to him. She let herself fall against his chest, hiding her face from the lifeless body that floated on the water behind her. "Baby, why didn't you tell me? You could have been killed." His eyes were moist.

"I knew you would stop me. I had to do this."

He just held her closer.

Chief Scheider shook his head at Rian. "I can't believe it, Mrs. Field. I want to reprimand you for taking on such a dangerous expedition, for not telling a soul, but I think you're more deserving of a reward." They all laughed. "By tomorrow morning, I will have a check made out to you and I will make sure that this makes the paper with your name on it, if, of course, you are okay with being personally identified as the hero who rid this town of a killer shark."

Rian smiled as she looked out at the black water. "Thank you."

By the next day, not only did the Chief keep his promise to write her a check, her name appeared in the papers too, specially edited by Floyd, making her sound like a world-class hero. Jack beamed at her as he filled two cups with black coffee from the kitchen. Champ's ears perked up as he looked at the newspaper. Jack reached down to scratch behind the Retriever's ears. "It's a good day, boy." He glanced over at Rian. "It's a very good day." She gazed at both of her boys, basking in the pleasure of being with them.

By the end of the month, Westen promoted her to Senior Marine Scientist. It wasn't always this way. Rian at the top of her game with a husband, and a career she'd only once been able to fantasize about. She was even able to forget about the masked men for a while. She and Jack were back to normal, the distorted past gone, replaced with lucidity and long overdue contentment.

Chapter Fourteen

Picking up some Chinese food on the way home from her first day in her new position, Rian felt safe in the car, like nothing and no one could hurt her. She placed the bags on the passenger seat, started the engine, and switched on the radio. A Led Zeppelin song was playing. She turned up the volume and started singing along. "The autumn moon lights my way. For now I smell the rain, and with it pain, and it's headed my way. Sometimes I grow so tired, but I know I've got one thing I got to do. . ."

As if on cue, the sky rumbled as deep gray clouds sailed across its surface, gathering in thick clusters. The thunder was followed by a bolt of lightning that shattered the air and tore open those clouds. A torrent of water burst through them and came tumbling down onto the car's windshield.

She switched on the wipers and they worked hard and fast as they swept back and forth across the windshield. Big bloated drops of rain flung against the glass. She squinted to see the road as she hunched over the wheel.

Robert Plant continued to belt out his feelings over the air waves and Rian was reminded of her dad, who had loved classic rock, in particular Led Zeppelin. She grew up learning the value of such music, surrounded by it almost every day. When her dad would ask her to help him in the garage, a classic song had to be playing. When they played cards or went fishing or whatever they did together, her dad insisted the music accompany them. For Rian, Led Zeppelin would always hold a special place in her heart.

As she continued driving through the deluge, she found pleasure and renewal in a baptism as rain swept furiously and urgently across the blurred window pane. The song also reminded her of who her dad had once been, a lively man with good taste and an appreciation for life. Rian needed to boldly embrace those values if she were going to get through this.

She and Jack enjoyed a nice dinner before the fireplace, listening to the exploding night as thunder continued its rampant rumbling. But by the time they went to bed, her body was on edge, as it usually was. "I feel like I'm just waiting to die," she told Jack.

"But you're alive, so live." He peeled back the sheets and pulled her next to him on the bed. She wanted to be able to do that, to just live. But how could she when she lived each day feeling like it would be her last?

Jack soon fell asleep, but she lied there for another hour, her body stiff with anxiety. When she finally fell asleep, she dreamed a horrible dream.

Those same fierce jaws that had tried to feast upon her came rushing toward her in the dream, its head swinging back and forth, its torso shuddering as it closed in on her. She shrieked under the water, her voice making a gagging, garbling sound as she dove deeper, aiming her body straight down toward the ocean bed, though it seemed unlikely that she could swim this far down, much less breathe without the proper swimming apparatus.

She dared not peer behind her for she knew she would only slow her pace. As she pushed herself away from the monster, she found herself moving into clearer waters. A soft glowing blue light was casting down a stark radiance as if emanating from a spotlight. At the bottom of the beam of light, curled innocently and unaware of any nearby danger, a tiny baby slept. She had to get to the baby before the shark did.

Managing to propel her body even faster, she sped toward the sleeping baby, scooped him up into her arms. And woke up. She was violently gasping as though still adrift in that nightmare ocean.

"Rian? My God, what's happened?"

At first, she didn't understand why Jack looked so concerned. Not until she looked down at her nightgown. It was saturated with ocean water. No, that wasn't possible. Her hands shined from the moonlight. It was just sweat, hot sweat, and it was plastered against her face. Her hair felt like a sticky mess and her nightgown was wet against her chest. But what was most concerning was the way her arms were wrapped around her torso as though she still held the baby from the dream.

"I had another dream about the shark and the baby, only this time, the shark was after me at first. I saw the baby below and I got to him and had him in my arms just as I woke up."

Jack went to the adjoining bathroom and returned with a wet washcloth that he used to brush her hair away from her forehead and dab at her face. He kissed her eyelids, her nose, then her lips as he cradled her in his arms. They sat on the bed with the moon sinking into its surrounding halo, spilling its light through the blinds onto their bodies, as if bathing them in a protectant shield. Just like the day on the beach when she'd been confident that she was about to encounter the shark, the certainty that the next and final phase of this living nightmare that had plagued her for over a year was about to be revealed. She believed more strongly than she had believed anything else that the masks were literally going to be taken off at last.

Chapter Fifteen

Summer 2016

Nearly six months had passed since Rian had experienced any nightmares. She had contacted the District Attorney's Office earlier in the summer, but they still were waiting for the DNA to come back on the cigarette. She didn't let the fact that it had been two and a half years bother her. Instead, she focused on what she did have. She found herself surrendering to Jack again and trusting him like she had before. Life was much better. No more nightmares, no more jumpiness.

All through the summer, she and Shonda kept busy on a new project. It kept them working long hours with very little time off, but neither of them complained. Jack was back to work too, full time, helping with the construction of a new lab for a local research facility.

The suspicion toward their friends, toward Jack, had vanished. She made it to the Fourth of July without any threat against her life. Jack thought a holiday party at their house would be good for them both, and she agreed. They were close enough to the fireworks show that they could all gather outside to watch them from their back yard. All of their friends came early to enjoy conversation and dinner before the big display at 9:00. Dylan and Shonda, Kristen and Sean, Randy, Floyd, Hal, and, best of all, Lilah and Luke.

"I told Luke we have to move here because I can't stand being so far away from my best friend." Lilah told her as Rian prepared her a shot of tequila and herself a glass of orange juice.

"And what did he say to that?"

"He agreed. His promotion was supposed to bring him out here months ago, but deadlines got pushed back. Now they're caught up for the most part. We'll know something next week."

She looked up in surprise. "Really? But. . . what about your job?"

"Already been approved for relocation."

"Lilah, I can't believe. . ." She nearly dropped the bottle as she raced around the bar to hug her friend. Lilah laughed as she hugged her back.

"We've been talking about it for some time now. It just isn't right that we live so far apart." She took ahold of Rian's hand. "I felt so guilty not being here with everything that happened."

Luke came up beside them, wearing his signature shades even though they were inside. For the first time since she'd known him, the fact that Rian couldn't read his expression bothered her. "I have a good feeling about this, Rian. I think the boss is gonna approve the move." As if sensing her discomfort, he took off his sunglasses and winked at her.

A hard cold feeling filled her lungs and battered her throat. She excused herself and hurried to the front door, opened it, and closed it behind her as she ran down the driveway. She stopped at the edge of the lawn and looked up at the darkening sky. Behind her, the door reopened and closed again. Someone walked softly through the grass. She turned.

"Sweetie, what's wrong? You ran out of there so fast. Someone upset you?" Hal placed his hand on her shoulder, his kindly eyes pure and true.

"Remember that feeling on the pier that I told you and Jack about? Like someone was close by?"

He nodded, a sad look washing over his face. "Is it back?"

"I don't know why." It had been months since she'd felt this way about anyone. She heaved her shoulders as she cried into his shoulder. He rubbed her back.

"Oh, Rian, oh sweetie. No one is going to hurt you, not with me here." She looked up at him and smiled. "Let me get Jack."

She stopped him. "No. I. . .I don't know if I can trust him."

She knew it seemed wrong to feel something so morbid about someone who had only loved her, but she also hadn't forgotten the confrontation between Jack and Randy a few months ago. Those doubts had abated for the last six months, but now they resurfaced.

"Has he done something to make you think he's behind that night?"

"I don't know how to explain it. Someone in there wants to hurt me. I can feel it. Someone close to me."

"Come back inside."

She nodded and followed him back to the living room.

Randy and Floyd were off in the corner, watching something on TV, though they seemed less engaged in the program than in the heated conversation they were having. Randy was doing most of the talking. From time to time Floyd glanced around the room as if he didn't want to be a participant. Rian wondered what they could be talking about that had them both so on edge.

"Ready for an appetizer?" Dylan interrupted her thoughts, balancing a tray of crackers and cheese.

"Sure," she said absentmindedly, not taking her eyes off the two men.

"Why don't you join us at the kitchen table? We're starting some blackjack."

Was Dylan deliberately trying to divert her attention because he knew something about the conversation? Or was it an innocent move encouraging her to have some fun? She wasn't sure, and that frustrated her. A bit reluctantly, she followed him to the table to where Shonda, Kristen and Sean were also seated. They looked up at her and seemed pleased that she was there. Before long, she found herself immersed in the game and forgot about her suspicion. In fact, she managed to enjoy the company and dropped back a couple more Tequila shots.

"Crank up the stereo!" Kristen shouted to Jack, who gladly obliged the request. An '80s station pumped out music and the house lit up on the inside with everyone's energy. Hal smiled at Rian from the next room. Randy and Floyd dispersed from their corner and were striking up a conversation with Jack at the bar. It didn't sound like a sinister discussion, but Rian couldn't be sure. Instead she decided to focus on the game, the music, her friends, and to purposely have fun to keep from losing herself to a cacophony of turmoil.

Right at nine o'clock, the first firework blew up in the sky. Everyone stopped the festivities and gathered to the backyard near the casita where they enjoyed a good view of the fireworks. The show turned out to be spectacular against the backdrop of the full silver moon, and soon Rian fell right back into her relaxed state. Kristen kept squealing at each blast of a rocket while Sean, usually quiet, cheered at the sparkling sights.

"Doing better, sweetie?" Hal tapped Rian's arm as he looked up at the sky.

Rian smiled. "This is my favorite holiday. It reminds me of my parents' years together, when they were happy, before my dad got sick."

Hal squeezed Rian's hand. "Don't forget Jack." He nodded over to where Jack was standing apart from them all. He looked withdrawn. She knew he wished she were standing right next to him, but he didn't want to push her past the point of comfort. Hal was right. She needed to go to him. If these two men were close by, right here, right now, then she better trust Jack. If he was involved, she would never trust him again. But if he wasn't, then her trust in him would reinforce their marital bond. It would also shield her from those who sought to further harm her. He turned aside as she moved up beside him and caught his hand in her own. "Having fun?" he asked.

"Not without you." She kissed his cheek and snuggled up next to him. A light chill drifted through the air as together they looked up at the fiery sky.

Afterward, Kristen and Sean decided to call it a night, but the others stayed behind, enjoying appetizers and drinks as Dylan flipped through the channels, searching for a late movie. Jack had gone to the bathroom when Floyd shifted his attention from the comedy Dylan stopped on, to her. As he made his way over to her in the kitchen he looked concerned in spite of his smile.

"Randy told me what happened between him and Jack at the Institute, that fight months ago. I didn't think it necessary to bring it up since it seemed to be over. But Randy says that lately Jack's been giving him the cold shoulder when no one's around, so maybe it's not really over."

"Nothing will ever be the same between them, I'm sure. But they can work it out eventually. Don't you think?"

"I think you're right." He paused as if hesitant to go on. "But Randy told me something that happened the other day between them." He looked behind him, outside, to where Randy and Hal were watching the leftover fireworks from local neighbors. He turned back to face her, a stone serious expression melting the smile from his mouth. "He told me not to tell you this, but I feel like I have to."

Rian did not like the direction of the conversation. She shifted slightly to the left to peer around Floyd. Randy's back faced her and he was nodding his head at something Hal was saying.

"Jack accused him of being there that night here at the house."

"What? On what basis?"

"Just the way things have been going between them, I guess. Really tense. Really uncomfortable. The trust is gone. He didn't even want Randy here tonight, but I convinced him to let him come."

"So why didn't Randy want me to know?"

"He's sure that Jack is just being emotional and is frantically seeking out the culprit. People say and do things they don't mean when they are feeling desperate."

She knew how valid that was. She'd mistreated Jack on more than a few occasions.

Floyd glanced behind him once again. Randy had disappeared. Hal was alone. "I better go."

A moment later, Jack returned to the kitchen, kissed her head, and looked in the refrigerator for some dip. "How's Champ?"

"Content in the closet."

"Oh, poor thing. I wish their ears weren't so sensitive so they could enjoy the show too."

She watched as Jack happily dipped some potato chips into the French dip and wondered how true Floyd's words were and why Jack hadn't bothered telling her anything. It wasn't like him to keep secrets. She needed to know what was happening.

"What's going on between you and Randy?"

"What do you mean?"

"I mean, things haven't been exactly friendly between the two of you for a while now."

Jack's neck stiffened as he swallowed the last piece of the chip and stared at her. "I don't think he's being honest."

"About what?" she asked.

"Something's off. I don't know what it is, but I think he's hiding something. I don't trust him. Not anymore."

"So why did you invite him?"

"I didn't. Floyd talked me into it." So, it was true. "Rian, I really don't want to talk about this. Let's just have a good time." He kissed her head again.

Hal had told her that Jack loved her and she wanted to believe it. He hadn't done anything to make her think she couldn't trust him. Except why did he suspect Randy? And why had Randy acted funny about Jack too? She remembered that day in the lab and other times when Randy had been a bit protective of her, and it was all too much. Her husband, their good friend, both accusing each other.

Jack went outside to Hal.

"Having fun?" Randy sidestepped Rian as she started to leave the kitchen. She turned around to see him twirling a red, white, and blue glow stick. But she wasn't in a fun mood.

"What in the hell is going on between you and my husband?"

"Rian, I really don't think now's. . ."

"Yes, it is. Now is the time. And I want to know what it is. What has you two going at each other, distrusting one another, accusing each other?"

The last remark made him shudder. "I didn't want to say anything. Not here." He looked out at the window, up at the stars. "I know you don't want to hear this, but I think he's involved."

"Don't you dare." Her voice was low, but her rage was building.

"He was there, Rian. Seconds after they left. He wants you to think he's innocent, but I know he's not."

"Get out!"

Shonda turned down the TV. "What's going on?"

"Nothing." Randy put down his drink and went out the front door. Jack came back inside. He took her hand. She shrugged it off and went to the spare bedroom and slammed the door.

A picture of Jack and her sat on the nightstand. In it, they were both laughing against a backdrop of a setting sun. The photo had been snapped by Lilah years ago in Virginia Beach. Long before the daunting moments. When there was total trust between her and Jack. She looked away from the memory and began to cry. It wasn't long before Jack came in.

"I love you. I don't know what this is about. I sent everyone home so we can talk about it. Can we do that?"

"I don't know anymore."

"OK." He took off his shirt and jeans and got into bed, his back facing her. "I have to work late tomorrow, so don't expect me until around midnight or so. I love you."

She was disheartened by how quickly he gave up. But she knew that was the end of the conversation. He always sealed talks with those three words, even when he was disappointed in her.

Rian slid under the sheets and lied on her back. She stared at the ceiling, watching the shadows of light from the moon churning and jerking back and forth. The movements reminded her of those of the shark in its final moments. She closed her eyes. Her mind began to drift to the beach and the positive things it had once meant. She wondered if that place of peace was gone forever. Seconds before she entered into the abstract realm of dreams, she made up her mind to spend the entire day there to find out.

Chapter Sixteen

The next morning, Rian woke up to find Jack already gone. The clock on the nightstand read 10:00. She was surprised she had slept so long, but her body felt relaxed and refreshed. Immediately she got dressed into tan khakis, a black t-shirt, and flip flops.

Up on the hall closet shelf was a long-forgotten wicker picnic basket that they used to bring on dates with Lilah and Luke. She pulled it down and went to the kitchen where she began busily humming an older tune, she couldn't remember who sang it, but she thought it might be Clapton. "I'm glad. I'm glad. I'm glad." And it was true, she really did feel glad. But it was more than that. She felt confident and in control of her life.

From the refrigerator, she withdrew a loaf of honey wheat bread, a package of beef bologna, and a jar of mayonnaise. She made two thick sandwiches. From the cupboard, she retrieved two small bags of potato chips. She tucked the food inside a cooler, adding a six-pack of bottled water, two cans of Pepsi, and two apples.

Back in the hallway she stooped at the lower cabinets and pulled out a deck of cards. She'd grown up an only child and had learned to self-entertain with solitaire. She smiled as she continued repeating the chorus of the song. "I'm glad, I'm glad, I'm glad." The house looked normal to her, not like a house that had once been taken over by two monsters. Not like a house where she had been violated.

Champ had been asleep on his bed near the fireplace, but now he got up and padded over to her. He sat at her feet, his head cocked, his ears perked. He softly whined.

"It's OK, boy. I'm just going to the beach to clear my head a little. I'll be back tonight. And so will Jack. Now just enjoy this big house all to yourself, but don't do anything I wouldn't do." She winked at him and scratched behind his ears. He whined, this time a bit louder as if to say he didn't buy the casualness in her voice. Rian sometimes pondered how much Champ understood the things they said.

Once, she had spoken aloud about wanting a piece of pie. Jack had just finished baking a homemade apple pie and it had been steaming on the countertop. A moment later, Champ was nudging the edge of the container with its nose. They figured he was just drawn to the delicious smell of the treat until what happened next. "What about my fork? I can't eat without a fork," Rian said. Champ had strolled over to the end of the counter and thrown up his paw on the silverware drawer.

She plopped down next to the Retriever and patted his golden coat. "I'm sorry things have been so confusing lately. But we'll get back to normal. I promise." He dropped his head into her lap and moaned. She rubbed his head and sighed. "I know."

Newport Beach was packed. Apparently, a majority of the city employees had taken off another day to deal with hangovers. Many of them were passed out on their stomachs, some leaning back in chairs with their heads lolled to the side, their eyes hidden beneath dark sunglasses. After making a second trip to the car for the cooler, she set up her things next to a lifeguard station and it made her realize how predictable she could be. She always parked her stuff near a lifeguard. She supposed it made her feel safer somehow.

The weather was severe, over a hundred degrees, though it wasn't yet quite noon. She was thankful she'd remembered to apply sunblock. She placed the picnic basket on the beach towel and opened up a big blue umbrella. It was something they'd purchased three summers ago, but they had never used it. She slipped her sunglasses on and lied down beneath the shade of the umbrella, letting the sun tickle the edges of her face. Soon, she dozed off, waking up hours later to discover that it was just after two. She had meant to eat lunch. Her stomach was gurgling.

From the cooler, she took out one of the bologna sandwiches, a bag of chips, and one of the Pepsis. As she ate, she enjoyed the views around her. Several body surfers were at play near the shore. A young man was running down the beach, his workout for the day. An older couple strolled the edges of the water, oblivious to the rest of the world. She took in a deep breath and could feel the salty water fill her lungs. As she finished the last bite of bologna, she fumbled through her beach bag and drew out a King novel, *The Shining*. She read it once before, in her college years, before Jack. She was looking forward to reading it again.

She sighed as she opened up to Chapter One and soon found herself escaping into the beginnings of a dangerous world, but one that was safe because nobody in the story could harm her. She was thankful to God, even though she never really had room for Him before.

By late afternoon, she had played ten games of solitaire, eaten the rest of the food she'd packed, and downed another bottled water. She was sitting close to the incoming tides, relishing the rolling surf as it painted the sand a metallic gleam. Sand-filled waves furled toward her feet, the diamond-coated water scattering into a body of white jagged veins. Above her, the half-moon waited for night. An unexpected wave pulled in. It was the high tide and it came rushing into shore, pounding the earth with a vicious slap and smearing the sand castles down into a murky mess.

Further up on the sand, the sidewalk lamps offered her just enough light to see. She took out the King novel again and read through several more chapters. But time passed by too quickly. When she next looked at her watch, she saw that it was just after midnight. She couldn't believe how late it was.

Apparently she had gotten pretty caught up in the story. She jumped to her feet. The lifeguards had already gone home at seven. The entire area was deserted.

In the ebony velvet heavens, the moon was sinking into its surrounding halo. Rian felt strangely isolated. A cold draft of salt water picked up and prickled the skin of her arms.

She quickly dug into her bag and pulled on her t-shirt and jeans. She wondered how Jack was doing, if he was more hurt by her rejection than she was. It pained her to doubt him. Suddenly, she realized she'd left her cell phone in the car. Jack always called her throughout the day, even when they were having problems. Anxious to get back to the parking lot, she shoved everything into the bag and folded up the umbrella, but like before she would have to make a separate trip to get the cooler. She hurried to the lot and threw everything into the backseat.

Her cell phone was wedged into one of the cup holders and she swiped it. Seven missed calls. All from Jack. She felt guilty. It wasn't like her to go the entire day without letting him know where she was. Of course, she hadn't deliberately hidden her whereabouts, but that didn't matter much when her life had been threatened on two occasions in less than two years. He was probably worried sick. He had left only two messages. In the first message, received just after one o'clock, Jack hoped she wasn't still asleep because it was such a beautiful day, a perfect day to go to the beach. Rian's heart skipped a few beats when she heard that for his words came across ominously, as if he expected her to be on the beach today. In the second message Jack was upset. It was left at six o'clock. "Well, it's me again, and you still haven't called. I know you're mad, but you don't need to ignore me. It isn't helping anything. Call me. Bye." No "I love you". Just "Bye."

Her heart sank like the moon in its sky. She bent over the steering wheel taking deep breaths. After a moment, she deleted the messages and returned the phone to the cup holder. She shoved the keys underneath the driver's seat. Why hadn't he called her again? It wasn't like him to be so cold. Didn't he care that it was midnight and she wasn't home? Didn't it concern him that she hadn't called him back?

She trudged back down the beach to get the cooler. She was just turning around to head back to the car when someone stepped in her path. The shadowy figure shrank back into the darkness, away from the street lamps.

"Jack, I'm sorry. I should have called."

He stepped forward. But it wasn't Jack. She started to smile. After all, he was her friend.

Chapter Seventeen

"He trains my hands for battle,
So that my arms can bend a bow of bronze.
You have also given me the shield of Your
salvation, And Your help makes me great.
You enlarge my steps under me,
And my feet have not slipped"
2 Samuel 22:35-37

"Hi, Rian." Randy's face was lit by the pale glow of the moon. His voice sounded funny, wrong. "What are you doing out here so late at night?"

"Just getting ready to go home."

But why did it seem like he was sneaking up on her? She quickly reminded herself that she was in control. That's what she had succeeded in doing during therapy. To no longer be the victim. To be the one who held the power. But he hadn't really answered her question.

"Why are you here?"

He looked at her. "To see you."

"How did you know I'd be here?"

"Because you're so predictable."

Oh God, just like she'd thought earlier today, when she'd situated herself next to the lifeguard, the way she always did. She was too easy to figure out, her every move so easily anticipated.

"I've been watching you. We knew how much you were struggling with the shark and how coming here would help you deal with it." *We?* "Once you killed it, I knew I could count on you to return to the place that meant so much to you."

She didn't know what he meant exactly until he took out a cigarette and lit it. A Lucky cigarette, the cigarette, just like the one from the crime scene. Oh God, oh Lord Jesus, it was him!

"You used to tell me this was where you came to clear your head." That's right. It wasn't like it was a secret. She assumed it was the most harmless thing she could have told him. She never thought it would be used to seek her out.

Too late, she wished she had called Jack back. At least he would know where she was. There were a few things she'd regretted in life. Not spending more time with her dad when he was well. Not knowing how to help her mom through his death. And not trusting Jack.

Randy reached out, took the cooler from her grip, and grabbed her arm. There was something in the motion that was horribly familiar. She jerked her hand away, but he was unfazed. "I highly advise that you come with me or this could get pretty scary for you."

Rian followed him down the beach, away from the parking lot and sidewalk lights and down by the rolling waves. It was high tide and the grunion were present, their shimmering turquoise bodies flopping against the wet sand, burying themselves into it as they prepared to lay their eggs. She wished she could hide too.

"Keep going," he told her as he pushed her forward.

"Why are you doing this?" she asked without turning around. She hoped that by maintaining a conversation she would remind him that she was human, that he was her friend, and that he wouldn't hurt her.

"You'll know soon enough," he promised.

She didn't like what she heard in his voice. Finality. Malice. She knew that he was planning to kill her. She didn't want to die. This was the only life she knew, even though it had been rough the past few years. But she was familiar with this world and she didn't want to leave it. Not yet.

Where was Jack? He'd said that he would be off around midnight. Wouldn't he come looking for her? She started to shiver as the spray from the ocean tingled against her legs.

"You got her?" Another male voice shouted from a few feet away, though it was much closer than she thought when a second later Floyd came into view, dressed in a tank top and shorts. The other half of *we*.

"Right here. Take care of Jack?"

"Yep."

"Where's Jack? What did you do to him?" she demanded.

"In due time, Rian. In due time," Floyd said.

Randy set down the cooler and pinned her arms behind her back. "Now you're going to know what real pain is."

"What are you doing?"

"Looks like we have to spell it out for her." Floyd tapped his finger against her forehead. "Don't you remember?" Then she knew as her eyes caught sight of his arm, in the area just above his elbow, a bright circular birthmark, like a drop of blood. She had somehow forgotten about it, but now she remembered. He had rolled up his sleeve and scratched at it when they first brought her into the house. The way they moved. The way they touched her. It was them. They were the ones that night who came into their house.

"No. Not you too." She looked at Floyd, then at Randy. Neither of them budged, but they both stared at her with tight grins, though Randy's dark eyes glared at her so hard that if it were possible, they would have drilled a hole through her skull. Floyd noticed her staring at his arm.

"The one mistake I made. I had to be pretty careful after you saw that. I couldn't just go around wearing short sleeves. I tell you, that got pretty hard to do, especially in the summer months." His mouth changed into a twisted smile. "You know, I was there during the earthquake. That was amazing, really, that an earthquake hit just moments before I threw the anchor into the house. You got shaken up in more ways than one, didn't you?" He smiled and it reminded her of the sneer of the Grinch from the Seuss cartoon. "It was my idea to do it. Something symbolic to reconnect you to the shark and put the fear back into you."

Randy glanced at Floyd and said, "She still doesn't get why. I guess it's time we explain." He smirked at her as he looked back, but it was a menacing smirk that chilled her heart. "When I found the test in your purse I finally knew why you'd been keeping secrets from me."

"What test? What are you talking about?" She was tired of his riddles.

He gritted his teeth. "You never met Jenna, but she looked a lot like you. She had the same mole in the same place as you do and that same damned strawberry blond hair. When I moved out here and met you and found out that we'd gone to the same school and all, I thought we had something special. You were so nice to me, like she was, but it was just an act. You thought you were better than me, just like she did, because you had a PhD. You betrayed me. Just like Jenna did." He grinded his teeth together and practically snarled those last words. And then he unbuttoned the top two buttons of his shirt. Shining under the moon's pale light across his dark toned chest were two words scrawled in black tattooed ink: Rian Field.

She shuddered and looked away. How could she have not known how sick he was? When she opened her eyes again, he buttoned his shirt back up and something changed in his face. In the light of the moon, she could see the blood rushing to his cheeks. He wasn't smiling anymore. Inside his eyes appeared something inhuman. He had created a delusion in his head, twisting reality to support the faulty narrative that Rian was Jenna.

"Fortunately, for us, we went for drinks after work. Remember? Dylan, Shonda, you, me, Floyd. Of course you remember. You'll always remember that night."

Floyd cut in. "I have my own personal lab. I gave you GHB—the technical term for it is Gama Hydroxybutyric Acid. It comes in a few different forms: odorless, colorless liquid, white powder or pill. The first form is personally my favorite because it reminds me of vodka, my favorite liquor, and at the most, it might give your drink a somewhat salty flavor. I mixed it in a glass of orange juice to mask the taste. We only had fifteen minutes for that to take effect. Dylan and Shonda had already left. Jack had just called to say he wouldn't be home for another three hours. We had to make sure you got home before you got too weak so we waited to give you the shot."

"It's all about the timing," Randy said as he winked at her.

"What were you trying to do?" She was furious.

Randy glanced at Floyd who explained. "The sleep induced by GHB is profound, similar to the state of a coma patient. Did you know that when a person is in a coma he experiences a reduced metabolic state which interferes with one's mental capacity? With the right dosage, that is, an overdose, one can potentially forget what happens to them during a few hours."

She couldn't believe what she was hearing. They had done something to make her forget. What could they have made her forget?

"And you helped him?" She looked up at Floyd. "Why?"

Randy answered for him. "I needed his medical expertise."

"You're an editor."

Floyd smiled as he shook his head. "That's just on the side. I'm a doctor. Randy and I grew up in Maryland together. We're best friends. He needed my help to get the job done." He shrugged. "What can I say? I'm a loyal friend. I was impressed with the impact of the drug. It doesn't always have such nice side effects. I had to give you a high dosage to ensure that you would forget what Randy had to do. And because it affects motor control it produces the perfect result of sleepiness. No, I take that back. Unconsciousness."

Randy took back over, his excited state a long black shadow of strangeness. "When you left to the bathroom that night at the restaurant, you left your purse on the table, wide open, and that's when I saw the test. You had already taken it. It was positive. Jenna got pregnant by someone else too when she was still dating me." He paused to look at her. Then he did something odd. He squeezed his hands together so tightly that his knuckles turned white. "When we got you to the house, I had a hard time holding back, but as soon as I could, right when the drug took effect, just after you fell asleep standing there against the wall, I socked you in the stomach and watched you sag to the ground. Jack would be getting there soon so we had to get you into your bed so it would like you had fallen asleep." He paused to take a breath. He was nowhere near done. His voice changed into one of cold-blooded rage. "I couldn't bear you giving life to a child, not without me. That baby should have been mine!" He screamed so hard that spit flew from his mouth.

Rian wobbled and Floyd balanced her. The dream about the baby and the blood. Now the missing piece could complete the puzzle. She bled for twelve days straight. Dark purple blood. The doctor said she'd lost the baby. She and Jack thought it had just happened naturally. But no. Someone had killed their baby. Oh, the pain of losing a child you never got to meet.

Rian almost fell backwards, but Floyd caught her. They had known all along. She was indignant. This. . .these vultures knew something so precious and had taken it from her. Oh, God. Now she believed in Him. He had to help her. They were both out of their minds. She had to figure out a way to escape.

The three of them stood near the ocean, the waves slapping the cold sand under the moonlight. It was horrifying to realize that he had knocked her down and that she had never felt it happening. After a time, she found her voice.

"I didn't know who you were. What did it matter if I was passed out?"

"The cops would have matched my DNA that much sooner if murder was involved, and I couldn't have anyone knowing about that," Randy said.

"Fortunately, I've dealt with a lot of miscarriages, so I knew that the bleeding would continue a few more days and that you would never link it to us being there, at least not directly," Floyd told her.

Tears started burning in the cavity of her heart. "Why now? Why, after all this time, do you decide to tell me now?"

Randy cut in. "At first, I tried to make it look like Jack was guilty, to turn you against him, and it worked. All I had to do was act like he was hiding something and you fell for it. But as the months went by, I became more haunted by how you betrayed me. I had to let you know what you had done. See, the GHB not only knocked you out, it created a temporary amnesia during that time. Only we could remind you of it. Consider it our gift to you." Here he paused and a strange smile crinkled his lips. "Since we'd already seen proof of what it could do in you, that glorifying night, we grew optimistic."

"What do you mean?"

Randy said, "That night in November last year. The shark attack on you wasn't an accident." He watched her as that information sunk in. "It was carefully planned. Once again, with Floyd's knowledge and willingness to comply, we were able to orchestrate this grand event. You see, I knew how much sharks meant to you, how terrified you still were of them, yet so desperate to overcome that fear. It was the perfect time to reinforce that fear."

Floyd said, "We numbed you, so to speak, with my own specially formulated GHB, back at the Institute. Remember, it was Randy's birthday and Shonda baked him a cake and made his favorite strawberry lemonade? It's so easy to slip the drug into someone's drink. Too easy."

"It was probably the best birthday gift I'd ever gotten, being there to watch you scream." Randy slowly turned his head to watch her. He explained how they had spent months navigating the waters, following a Great White, watching for patterns. Randy had to disable the Institute's receiver. But once they outfitted their own private transmitter to track the shark, they were able to time its whereabouts perfectly and ensure that it would be there. He was more than happy to explain how they used fish uncommon to those waters as bait to lure it.

"It worked sometimes," Floyd added, "but usually the shark showed no interest, not until we tried the dolphins. See, Randy here paid attention to what Shonda's team was doing at the Institute. Once we saw its success, we utilized them for that night. They were these dolphin-shaped cardboard cutouts we used as decoys, attempting to lure you to your death on the pier."

Randy shoved his face close to hers, his hands pressed atop her shoulders. "The shark was a bit angry, you see, what with all the teasing we did to it as you lied helplessly in the Sundancer. It didn't much appreciate us dangling phony fish. By the time you became conscious again, it was seeking vengeance."

Floyd took over. "While you were passed out, we lassoed the sucker and flipped it upside down. We had to be quick as it was starting to go into a catatonic state. I made a small incision and inserted the tag. We were able to track it from the comfort of my home."

"We did regret a bit attacking an innocent life, but it was important to eliminate any suspicion that it was personal. Hurting Jimmy Woods was a necessary red herring; it couldn't look too obvious that someone was out to get only you. Indeed, it produced the desired effect. You wanted justice.

Your individual pursuit of the fish led you right into our trap. You see, you believed it was over, the nightmares, the stalking, and you started to trust again. You were so determined to find the shark, so vulnerable, that turning you against Jack was a simple task. It was satisfying in more ways than one—it broke your trust in your husband and made you a crazy wreck while strengthening your trust in me," Randy said as he let go of her and looked at her with disgust.

By the time they finished their sick story, all she could feel was an intense level of bitterness. What they said explained her strange connection to the shark, why it had reminded her of that night. They had been linked. Intricately and intimately intertwined. She wasn't frightened or paralyzed by the revelation, but she was angry at the stealth by which they pulled it off.

Floyd added, "You know what's truly inspiring though? The fact that we were all together that day with Koontz and the photographer, another one of your shining moments, and then here comes the shark, without any planning, without our influence or manipulation, a beautiful symphonic dedication to our work."

Randy swallowed hard and glowered at her. "You got what you deserved, Rian. And now comes the finale." Randy reached behind his back and pulled out a knife. A KA-BAR. *Her* KA-BAR.

She wasn't afraid of him. Not this time. "How did you get that?"

Floyd smiled, no longer attractive. His dark striking features were now just dark. "I'm very resourceful. Remember, I was a contributing editor on the story about the team. Those scientists were killed, but not because of the shark. They never even tracked the shark. I tampered with their equipment beforehand to ensure that wouldn't happen. I had to make up that story that they'd been attacked by the shark so that no one ever went looking for them. But what really happened was far more interesting. The team was feeling pretty confident that day and we all went celebrating on the boat. Thankfully, no one else would ever discover that I had been there too. It was a last minute invite on their behalf. You know what else is so incredible about it? How easy it is to slip a drug in someone's drink. Within twenty minutes, they were all passed out. Five minutes after that, I had them all secretly submerged in the water. Nobody ever found out that they drowned."

Rian felt sick. She started to back away, but Randy grabbed her, wrapping his arm around her throat. The same hold he'd used on her two and a half years before.

Floyd wasn't done. "Koontz trusted me to do the write-up on your final meeting with the shark as well. I simply went inside the storage area where they were temporarily holding the shark, as Koontz instructed me to, so that I could gather more information. No one noticed the missing knife until the next day, you know, the one you used to try to kill the shark. By then, a number of people had come and gone, so pinning the missing knife on me would be difficult."

Randy cut in. "We had to make sure that you faced your demons. You had to be the one there with the shark. It would bring closure for you. I wanted your final moment with the shark to be one you would never forget."

"For whatever it's worth, I did try to help you remember. It was the day after it happened. We were at your house, you were making cookies, and I tried to get you to think it was someone you knew."

She couldn't believe how happy he looked as he said this, acting as though he had done her a favor. But Randy wasn't in a cheerful mood nor did he try to be.

"I hated you for making us wait so long. If you'd just listen from the start, paid attention to what we were trying to tell you, I could have had closure much sooner."

Randy pointed the tip of the weapon at her. It gleamed like an opaque arm of death. To Floyd, he said, "Meet me back at the car."

Floyd jogged off toward the north part of the parking lot, which was flanked by palm trees, in the opposite direction from where she'd parked. She was glad she left the keys in the car. One less thing they could take from her. Randy stepped toward her. The spray from the ocean sent a shiver through her and she hugged herself, her hands tucked inside her shirt. He pushed her around so that she faced the ocean. "Move."

Underneath her shirt, she felt the cold touch of the necklace against her fingers. She tugged on it and yanked it down until the cool stones rubbed against her palm.

She and Randy were in the water now. The temperature was frigid and her teeth were clacking together. She fiddled with the chain until she had it crumpled up into a ball.

"Turn around," he commanded.

The knife reflected off the cold darkness of his eyes. "It's time to say goodbye to this world." He brought the knife up and tilted it so that the blade pressed into her shoulder. She jerked back. "Hey!"

In one fast motion, she let the chain dangle from her hand, swung it upward, and slashed at his face. He cried out. The diamonds had cut into his eyes and blood was running down his face.

She made a run for the parking lot but was grabbed from behind.

"Not so fast." Randy violently spun her around and she nearly fell to her knees. "I've been patiently waiting for this moment. You are not going to take it from me."

"No!" She tore away from his grip and attempted to run, but he was too fast. He pushed her down into the sand. It felt rough and cold against her cheek. He pressed his foot onto her back. She moaned in pain.

"Are you done running? Cause I've already caught you and there's nowhere for you to go. Now, if you'll stop playing this game, I'll let you up."

She nodded and he yanked her up so that she was face to face with him. She could feel his hot breath on her chin; it smelled of peppermint. His cheeks were wet with blood. The pendant had sliced some of the skin underneath his eyes.

He looked down at the water and back to her, then back at the water as if deciding on a course of plan. What was he plotting now? To drown her? She shivered and looked down the beach, hoping someone might be out for a late night stroll.

"It's just you and me, Rian," he said, as if sensing her thoughts. "I've got a new idea about what I'm going to do with you. It's a better plan that I had originally thought. But I need to get Floyd." He let go of her for a second and that's when she took action.

She dashed to her car, pumping her arms as fast as she could. Within seconds, she was behind the wheel. The engine started right up. In the next second, Randy's face was at the driver's window, his brown eyes black in the night's light.

"Where do you think you're going!" he yelled.

Before she could react, he reached in through the open window, turned off the car, and pulled the keys out of the ignition. "Get out."

Reluctantly, she opened the door and stood on the pavement beside him. She must think fast. Perhaps there was a hint of sanity left somewhere inside of him. Maybe, if she got through to him somehow, he would realize that his motives weren't reality. If she could just get him to see that maybe her life could be spared. It was her last hope. "I'm not Jenna, Randy. I did nothing to you. I'm Rian, your friend. Your trusted friend."

His eyes were wild and he raised the knife into the air, waving it around. "You did everything! You were supposed to be mine!"

Rian knew there was no reasoning with him anymore. He was gone. Completely gone.

He shoved her toward the beach, the knife at her throat. "You're going to pay for what you did." His voice was deadly. The point of the blade pinched her skin as they came near the water.

Another voice shouted, "Back away!"

Randy spun them around and gasped. "Jack! How the hell did you get out? Floyd had you tied up."

"Put the knife down." Jack was holding a pistol, their Colt 1911 .45. They had used it only once, three years ago, for target practice. Now he was aiming it right at Randy's chest.

Randy said, "Put the gun down and I'll think about putting the knife down."

Jack didn't waver. He held the gun steady.

The rolling surf whooshed behind them. A small circle of moonlight, partially hidden behind the grey film of clouds, intercepted the darkness.

"Put it down," Jack repeated.

"Sure, Jack." Instead, Randy pushed the blade deeper into her neck. In the next moment, everything happened in a blur of commotion. Jack lunged forward. BANG! The gun went off, right at Randy's head. He dropped the knife and fell on his back. Jack slid the gun into his pants pocket and hurried over to Rian's side. He took off his jacket and pressed it down onto her neck where a small gash was leaking blood. He went back over to where Randy lied on his back and checked his pulse.

"He's dead." Returning to Rian, he gently helped her up. "We need to get to the car. Quickly."

"The keys. Randy took them."

He searched Randy's pockets and pulled out the keys.

Holding one another's hand, they started across the sand.

"Freeze!" Floyd was back. And with a gun, some kind of rifle. He looked like a mad- man. He aimed the gun at Rian.

Click! Jack jumped before the fire and the bullet slammed into his chest. He fell into the sand, next to Randy.

"No!" Rian cried out. She wanted to go to Jack, but she couldn't turn her back on Floyd. From the corner of her eye, she detected the knife partly buried in the sand, mere inches from her feet, opposite Floyd, who was hovering over her. He looked taller than ever.

Floyd said, "Randy, it's time." He glanced over at his friend. "Randy?" He lowered the gun and walked over to his body where he stooped beside him. Floyd made a strange guttural sound. "Randy?"

Rian knelt beside Jack. A small amount of blood was oozing from his chest. No. She didn't want to live this life without him. He had to be all right. She leaned in close to his ear and whispered his name. He didn't respond. But she heard something else—his shallow breathing. He was alive! But this wasn't over yet. They were still in danger. Inside Jack's jacket, she found his cell phone and called the police.

"What are you doing?" Floyd whipped around.

"Yes, I need two ambulances and the police. Newport Beach, near the east parking lot. One person is dead. Floyd Henderson, the editor of the local paper, is trying to kill me. He's already shot my husband, Jack. Please hurry." She dropped the phone to the sand. She needed both hands now.

Floyd took a step toward her, swinging the rifle.

The knife was right next to her. She scooped it up, lunged toward Floyd, surprising him, wrestled the rifle away from him, dropped the knife, and pointed the gun at his chest. He stopped.

Five minutes later, three units pulled into the parking lot, their sirens wailing. Floyd held up his hands in surrender. A deputy handcuffed Floyd. Randy was pronounced dead and the paramedics carried his body off on a gurney and into an ambulance. She rode with Jack in the ambulance to the hospital.

Chapter Eighteen

"Into the darkness
  Cold vengeance drifted
  Her heavy heart
  Now slowly lifted"

Jack spent a week in the hospital. He was fortunate that the bullet bounced off his rib cage. The bullet had fractured a rib, but it was expected to heal within the next six weeks. The doctors monitored his vitals until his shallow breathing returned to normal. His wound soon healed and the bleeding stopped. He left the hospital wearing a stabilizing elastic binder to help the healing of his ribs by keeping his chest from expanding. They were extremely grateful he had survived. Grateful to God.

The Newport Beach event made headlines. The story of the shark attack on the scientists was reversed once the video was discovered in Floyd's house, showing what had really transpired. The newspaper also covered another memorable story; Rian Field would be receiving a special medal from Mayor Koontz himself in recognition for her bravery and her search for the truth.

When Jack returned home, Hal brought over a chocolate strawberry cake with the words "Jack and Rian—Heroes" decorated across the top. He hugged them both close to him and shed tears of happiness at their survival. Champ was not forgotten. Hal also brought with him a special chew toy for the Retriever. Sean, Kristen, Dylan and Shonda spent the first night with them as well. At first, the mood was solemn, but Dylan soon found a way to make everyone laugh. Best of all,

Lilah and Luke found a house just down the street from them, which meant many nights of games, movies, and fun.

But these moments were bittersweet. The discovery of what happened to their baby hit them in an agonizing way. They cried and held each other, mourning the murder of their child. The pain did subside as the weeks went by, at least to a certain degree. With their friends close by, the pain of what happened was that much more bearable. The curtain of terror and doubt had fallen. Life was slowly becoming wonderful and livable again.

After six months went by, she and Jack agreed it was time to take a much needed vacation. They'd had enough of the ocean for a while, so they decided to get away to Las Vegas. They spent the first two days playing the slot machines, coming away with a modest winning. The rest of the week they spent mostly in bed, enjoying one another, watching movies, eating junk food. And by the end of their getaway, Rian had something important to tell him.

"I'm pregnant."

"I sought the LORD, and He answered me, And delivered me from all my fears." Psalm 34:4

Krista Wagner, a mother of three and wife of TJ, has been writing since she was seven. She started out writing songs and plays and then graduated to poetry during her teen years. In high school, she was on the staff of her literary magazine, co-authored her own zine, and began to write numerous short stories, mostly dealing with dramatic instances like murder or kidnapping.

Krista received her BA in English from UMBC in 1999, her MA in English Composition with a Literature Concentration from CSUSB in 2008, and an MFA in Creative Writing from National University in 2013. Since 2008, Krista has been an English adjunct instructor.

In 2012, Krista started work on her first novel, *Intent*, and completed it during a summer road trip in 2013. *Intent* was published with TouchPoint Press in 2014. Her upcoming novel, *The Gold*, a middle-grade fantasy, is scheduled for a Summer 2016 release. She has also penned screenplays for her published novels. She enjoys suspenseful films, reading the Bible, and spending time with her family.

If you enjoyed this book, I hope that you will take the time to post a review on Amazon and spread the word. My readers are the ones who keep this story alive.

Connect with the Author:
kristawagner.wix.com/rian-field
rianfield.blogspot.com/p/blog-page.html
www.facebook.com/RianField821536817900715/
https://twitter.com/krista73818799
https://www.goodreads.com/book/show/28369964-rian-field

Made in the USA
San Bernardino, CA
13 July 2016